FALLEN FROM GRACE

FALLEN FROM GRACE

By
J. R. Lindermuth

Oak Tree Press  Taylorville, IL

Oak Tree Press

Oak Tree Press books may be purchased for educational, business or sales promotional purposes. Contact Publisher for quantity discounts.

First Edition, March 2011
10 9 8 7 6 5 4 3 2 1
Cover by Lewis Agrell
Text Design by Linda W. Rigsbee

ISBN 978-1-61009-011-7
LCCN 2011923693

DEDICATION

For my own Lidia

OCTOBER 5, 1897

CHAPTER 1

Clink.

Repetition of the sound roused me from a deep slumber. I jumped up, peering round the dark room, trying to recollect my wits and focus on what had disturbed my sleep. The sound came again. I inhaled fusty air and snorted. Then, throwing my feet out from under the quilt, I crossed the cold floor to the window and flung up the sash. A blast of frosty air helped revive me.

Leaning out, I peered into the dark yard. Though I couldn't make out who or what, a movement below caught my eye. "Who's there?" I bellowed. "Whatdya think you're doin' throwing pebbles at my window? You could have broke the glass."

A slim figure moved out from the house and was bathed in just enough moonlight for me to see him. "Sorry, Sheriff. It's me, Simon Hinkle. Doc says to fetch you."

The boy worked for Doctor Mariner and if he wanted me it could only mean trouble. I told Simon to wait while I got some clothes on. I shut the window and grunted. You don't get to be the law in a small town without expecting to be woke from your sleep every now and again. But that doesn't make it easier to bear. Especially not in the middle of a chilly autumn night.

I found my shirt and pants without lighting the lamp but managed to stub my toe before locating my shoes and socks. A few choice phrases helped ease the pain.

Shrugging into my coat and pulling a stocking cap down over my ears, I went out to where the boy waited. "What is it? What's the problem?"

"Doc's tending a man was stabbed," Simon said, leading the way across the yard.

There was no need of a conveyance. Hiram Mariner lives just across the road from me. Lights blazed through the windows of his office at the side of the big frame house where he lives with his wife, two near-grown daughters and young Simon, an orphan boy he has kindly taken in.

Pulling the coat closer around me, I followed. The air bit at exposed flesh and, glancing up, I saw stars sparkling against a dark sky. A near full moon was descending off to the west. As we stepped up on Doc's porch an owl saluted the moon's setting.

Simon opened the door and moved aside for me to enter first. Mariner was bent over a figure on the operating table. His wife, Clara, a tray of instruments in her hands, glanced over at me and nodded.

"How is he?" I asked.

"Can't say for sure just yet," Doc said without turning from his work. "Why don't you have a seat in reception and I'll get to you soon's I can."

"There's coffee on the stove in the kitchen," Clara said. "Simon, get the sheriff a cup and then come back here to help us."

Simon led me into the waiting room and I found a seat while he went for my coffee. "Just black," I hollered after him. "And if Miz Mariner has any cookies out there bring me some of them, too."

It never fails to amaze me how the reception room always has a pleasant odor unlike the anesthetic stench of the surgery. Even now, sniffing the air, there was a mingling of Clara's lilac perfume with a hint of something else, a bouquet reminding me of fresh-baked bread.

I loosened my coat, leaned back and shut my eyes. Seemed to me Doc could have waited until he was done to call me. But he isn't the patient type and I supposed he wanted me there and handy as soon as he was ready for me.

We Tilghmans have been sheriff here in Arahpot for three generations. My daddy, his daddy before him, and now me. The pay isn't anything to brag about but, usually, the work isn't too strenuous. The only alternatives around here are farming and working on the railroad, neither of which particularly appeal to me. Since I'm still single (and bound to remain so unless I ever convince Lydia Longlow to marry me) and my house passed down to me mortgage-clear, I don't have need for a whole lot of money. Not that I would turn down a raise, mind you. But a man has to be practical.

I was mulling these thoughts when the boy returned with my coffee and a handful of molasses cookies. I took them, nodded at him gratefully and bit into a cookie as he went on into the other room.

A clock ticked in another room and I heard the murmur of Hiram's and Clara's voices, though I couldn't make out what was said.

I'd finished the coffee and the last of the cookies and was wishing for more of the latter when Doc came through the doorway, wiping his hands on a white towel. There was blood splashed across the front of his shirt and a smear on one cheek. His eyes looked tired behind thick glasses and his thin face was drawn and sallow.

"How is he?" I asked, rising to meet him.

"Remains to be seen. Lost a lot of blood before he got to me." He sank into a chair next to mine, so I resumed my seat.

"Who is he?"

"Don't know. Clara's done cleaning up in there you can have a look, see if you recognize him."

"How'd he get here?"

"Teamster found him on the road out by the new bridge."

"South side of town?"

Mariner nodded. "Fellow loaded him on his wagon and brought him straight here."

"This teamster have a name?"

"Ollie Cramer. You know him."

My turn to nod.

"Told him to go on home and get some rest. Figured you could talk to him later, though I don't know how much more he can tell you than what I already did."

"I'll still need to talk to him."

I heard a stirring then and Clara stepped into the room followed by

Simon. "We're going back to bed, dear, unless you need anything more."

"No. You go on ahead. I'll sit with our patient."

"Doc," I said, rising, "you look about to collapse yourself. Why don't you go with your missus and I'll stay with the fellow."

Mrs. Mariner gave me a grateful look but Doc wasn't ready to relinquish full control yet. "I'll just lay down on the parlor sofa for a few winks," he said. "If the patient stirs you come get me, you hear?"

"Will do."

I stepped into the other room and had me a look at our victim. First glance I thought he looked vaguely familiar though I couldn't place just where I'd seen him. I stepped up for a closer look.

Then it dawned on me and my mouth gaped open wide enough to catch flies.

CHAPTER 2

"You're sure he's the same man?" Doc asked as Clara served us breakfast later that morning.

Pausing long enough to swallow my chunk of biscuit, I nodded. "It's him. I recollect because I took a good long look after seeing the expression on Valentine Deibert's face. I don't remember ever seeing so much fear on a person's face. I've heard of people going white in the face. But I never witnessed it before."

Doc was jellying a biscuit. He laid aside his knife and looked up at me. "Did you ask him about it?"

"Sure did. Told me I was mistaken, that he'd never seen the man before."

"What about..."

"Never got the chance just then. Man was out of the store and disappeared before I got out the door to look for him. I did talk to him later, though."

Clara paused in pouring me coffee and she and Hiram both stared at me, waiting for the rest of the story.

Man telling a tale has to keep his audience in anticipation. I took my time, delaying long enough to slide a couple more eggs and a rasher of bacon onto my plate before continuing. I noticed Simon and the two

Mariner daughters sat with their implements poised in the air, too. Finally, Emma, the prettier of the two girls, prodded me to go on. Emma has got her mother's blue eyes and the same fair complexion. I suspect she has a bit of a crush on me and, if my interest wasn't so fixed on Lydia, I might consider... Well, anyway, I went on.

"I found him down at Buchner's livery. And I asked him what his business was in our town. He gave me a sour look as though inclined to smart off. Then he changed his mind and said he was just passing through."

"But you didn't believe him, did you, Sheriff Tilghman?" asked Sissy, the elder Mariner daughter who is plain faced and a bit skinny like her father.

"No, I didn't, Miss Sissy. But there was no adequate reason for me to go calling the man a liar or twisting his arm to make him tell the truth."

"So what did you do, Sheriff?" asked Simon.

I took a minute to sample the bacon and wash it down with a swig of coffee. A dog barked outside and there was a banging of the shutters in the wind that had come up over night. "I asked if he knew Mister Deibert. He let on like he didn't know who I was referring to. I reminded him it was the man he'd bumped into at the store. He looked me right in the face and swore he'd never laid eyes on Valentine before."

"You don't think Deibert's the one stabbed him, do you?"

I pondered a moment, giving Hiram my full attention before replying to his question. "No, I don't," I said, shaking my head. "Deibert's a lot of things, but I don't think he's the kind to go around stabbing people."

Simon, seated at my elbow, giggled. "I don't think Mister Deibert could get close enough to stab a man."

The remark earned him a scowl from Clara but I was inclined to agree with the boy despite the unkindness of his comment. Valentine Deibert had enough trouble just waddling across a room. I didn't see him working up the energy, let alone the meanness, to stick another man with a knife. Still I would have to talk to him. The look on his face that day in the store, I knew both men lied about their previous acquaintance.

"Did you happen to find out our victim's name?" Hiram asked. "There was no identification in his clothes."

"Told me his name was Runkle. Conrad Runkle. Said he came from down in Lancaster County. Whether any of that's true, your guess is as good as mine. When do you think he'll be up to talking to me?"

Mariner drained his coffee cup and gestured with it for one of the girls to fetch the pot for a refill. Sissy took it upon herself and after she'd poured for her father I held out my cup for more. She'd filled my cup and returned to her seat before Hiram answered my question.

"As I said, he's lost a lot of blood. I patched him up as good as I could but I can't say he'll recover. He was still unconscious when I looked in before breakfast. We'll just have to wait and see."

"Well then," said I, taking a sip of my coffee and casting an envious look at the last biscuit on the plate between us, "maybe I should head out to Deibert's and see what more I can learn there."

Clara reached out and pushed the plate with the biscuit across to me. "Why don't you take that to eat on the way, Sylvester. It's a cold morning and a big man needs lots of fuel to keep himself warm."

Grateful for her kindness, I snatched up the biscuit and gave her a nod. "I'll be on my way then. See you all when I get back."

****

Since it was on the way, I stopped first to see Ollie Cramer. The teamster wasn't happy to be rousted from his bed so early in the morning but he answered my questions quick enough. And, as Doc Mariner had predicted, there wasn't much he could add to what I already knew.

I thanked the man and let him get back to his bed.

****

Arahpot isn't much of a town. But I was born and raised here and it suits my needs. Once it had been the seat of Jordan County, Pennsylvania. That was long before my time. The honor has since gone to Shannon, which is a much bigger and progressive city—thanks to the thriving anthracite coal industry. Let them have the dubious honor I say, and the troubles which go with it.

Being on the very border of the coal country, we profit from it but much more from agriculture—which to my way of thinking is not only cleaner but more reputable.

I've been offered more than once a job on the Shannon police force. And I'll keep on declining if ever I'm asked again. Even though it would mean more money, I'm sure it would equal in troubles. Besides, it would keep me from seeing Lydia on a daily basis and that's something I truly treasure even if she never consents to be my bride.

An advantage to being a law enforcement officer in a small town like Arahpot is you not only know everybody you also know much of their business.

Valentine Deibert was an exception to that rule.

He and his family had arrived in Arahpot about six months ago. They were cordial when met but not the most sociable people you'd ever want to encounter. They were an odd assortment and, naturally, aroused a certain amount of gossip in the community—most of it based on little more than speculation. Still they hadn't caused any trouble and I was content to accept their eccentricity if that was the way they wanted to live.

Deibert was a man in his mid-fifties, grossly obese and with obvious problems in breathing and moving about. He'd purchased the Philip Schneider farmstead after the old man passed away and hired Schneider's youngest son, Henry, as tenant to work the land for him. Though no one was going to get rich off that land he appeared to have ample means for his family's support.

His wife was a pert little thing half his age. She wasn't the kind of girl who'd have poems or songs written about her but she was nice enough looking to have tongues wagging about why she would marry a man like him. Verbena Deibert seemed quiet and shy and content with her lot.

The third member of the family was his sister, Catherine, a woman nearer his own age and as thin as he was stout. She wore her gray hair in a tight bun and folks said her lips were stretched just as taut. I'd never had dealings with her but Lydia claimed she was short-tempered and mean as a copperhead caught in the henhouse.

I got down from my rig, hitched my horse to the gate post and walked up to the front door. I thought I'd seen a curtain twitch at the front window as I drove up. But no one responded to my first two knocks. I bent and tried to peep through the curtains. They were drawn too close. The wind was still up, flinging dust and rattling tree branches against the house. Maybe they just hadn't heard me. I went back and pounded on the door some more.

I was just about to give up when the door drew open just a crack.

"Yes?" a meek little voice asked.

Through the opening I could see Verbena eying me. I swept off my cap. "Good morning, Mrs. Deibert. It's Sheriff Tilghman. Is your husband to home?"

"Mister Deibert is indisposed," she said and started to close the door.

Lucky for me, I have a big foot. I stuck it in the opening and prevented her closing me out. "I'm afraid I've got to bother him, ma'am. Will you let me in?"

With apparent reluctance she slowly opened the door. Eyes lowered, she murmured, "He's feeling poorly. My husband suffers from gastroenteritis, you know."

And a half dozen other ailments common to the practiced hypochondriac, according to town gossips. "Sorry to hear that, ma'am. I wouldn't be bothering him if it wasn't important. Can you fetch him?"

"If I must," she said and sighed. "Come inside." She led me down the hall and directed me to the parlor. "I'll go and see if he's up to it."

I stepped into the parlor and found Reverend Leonard Huber, the Methodist pastor, seated on the sofa, books and papers strewn across a marble-top table before him. Catherine Deibert was seated opposite him in an armchair, a clutch of knitting in her boney hands. Both scoured me with eyes that didn't veil their irritation at my interruption of whatever had been in progress.

"Sheriff," the minister said, rising and bobbing his head in my direction.

"I suppose you'll be wanting coffee," Catherine said, springing up and tossing her yarn on the chair. She rustled on by me without awaiting my reply and disappeared through the doorway by which I'd entered.

"Have a seat," Huber said, resuming his own.

I didn't want to sit on the lady's knitting so I settled onto a hardback chair by the fireplace. With no fire lit there was a chill to the room which made me glad for my overcoat. As usual, Huber was decked out in a dark, double-breasted suit and had a black silk tie under the high collar. I knew on his salary the suit had to be a cheap one. Still it was a sharp contrast to my country-bumpkin coat, denim shirt and corduroys. I removed my cap and twisted it in my hands.

There was a rustle at the door and Mrs. Deibert came in. I noticed she wore a purple wrapper that went well with her complexion. She exuded a strong but not unpleasant scent as she passed by me and seated herself beside the minister. "My husband will be down directly," she said.

"Your sister-in-law went to prepare coffee," Huber told her.

Mrs. Deibert raised her eyes to meet mine. "My husband is a most kind man," she said, pointing to the books and papers. "He knows my education was neglected and he's taken steps to improve my knowledge."

"He's hired me as tutor," Huber said, flashing a smile that displayed bad teeth.

"That's very generous of him," I said, adding, "I'm not here to question his kindness."

"Then why are you here disturbing us?" came a raspy voice from behind us.

CHAPTER 3

Deibert came forward, his heavy step causing the shade on the lamp to quiver and vibrating the window panes.

I swiveled in my seat to face him and saw he'd flung a banyan over his nightgown which was stained down the front with some brown substance I didn't care to know about. His flushed cheeks quivered as he huffed through his mustache. He floundered across the room and dropped into the chair previously occupied by his sister. He squirmed a moment, then reached behind him to draw out her knitting, which he dropped to the floor beside him. "What's so all-fired important you had to raise me from my sick-bed, Sheriff?"

Gazing at him, again I doubted his ability to inflict harm on any man. Still I had to ask my questions. "Recall the man who bumped into you at the general store the other day?"

"The man you insisted I knew when I swore I'd never laid eyes on him before that day. What about him?"

"Someone has stabbed him. Perhaps killed him."

Mrs. Deibert gasped.

"Dear Lord," said the pastor.

Deibert grunted. "And you think I done it?" He ran pudgy fingers through the scant gray hair awry on his scalp.

I shook my head. "No, sir. But I think you do know him."

"Is the man dead?" Reverend Huber asked.

"Not as of this morning. But he's been badly hurt and Doc Mariner says the man's fate is in hands greater than his."

"Are you calling me a liar then, Sheriff?" Deibert asked, heaving himself forward in his chair.

Before I could reply we were interrupted by the return of his sister. Huber pushed the clutter aside and she sat the tray she carried down on the marble-top. "Who wants coffee?" she asked.

"I'd be grateful," I said, anxious to delay a full-out confrontation with Deibert. My bladder was already complaining about its previous complement of coffee and I didn't really need more.

"Get me some milk, will you, my dear," Deibert instructed his wife. "Coffee won't do with my stomach. Help yourself, Reverend. Catherine, are there any more of those gingersnaps? Perhaps Reverend Huber would enjoy some of those.

I didn't expect the man to be hospitable under the circumstances but I might have liked some of those cookies, too.

Deibert still leaned forward, wheezing and with bulging eyes fixed on me.

I accepted a cup of coffee from his sister and stood facing him. "I wouldn't want to be so blunt as that, Mister Deibert," I said, "but the look on your face..."

"He startled me. Nothing more."

"Then you're sayin' you never saw him before that day?"

"That is what I told you that day and what I hold to on this." He leaned back, took a deep breath and grunted.

I returned to my seat and took a sip of the coffee. It was weak stuff. Nothing so good as Clara Mariner's. Hopefully the cookies would be better. Deibert and the minister were waiting for me to continue, so I did. "The man's name was Runkle. Conrad Runkle. Mean anything to you?"

I thought I detected a quick glance between Deibert and his sister, but I could have been mistaken. At any rate, he didn't change his tune. "No. I told you I didn't know the man."

"He came from down in Lancaster County. Didn't you come from down that way, too?"

"We lived in Dauphin County before we came here," Catherine Deibert said. There was an edge to her voice gave me a sense of the temper Lydia had mentioned.

Mrs. Deibert came back with a glass of milk for her husband and a plate of cookies. She gave them to the minister as her husband took the milk from her. I was about to ask Huber to pass the cookies when Verbena spun on me. "Can't you see my husband is ill? Must you pester him now?"

"It's all right, my dear," Deibert said, reaching out to pat her hand. "The sheriff is just doing his job."

"But he's upsetting you."

"It'll be all right. We have nothing to hide."

Verbena knelt then and laid her head on his lap. The sight of it flustered me and I decided there was no use prolonging the situation. I wasn't going to get the truth out of Deibert without more ammunition. I sat aside that bad-tasting cup of coffee and rose. All eyes turned on me.

"Well, Mister Deibert, if you say you never met the man I guess I'll have to accept your word. I won't trouble you no more today. I hope you feel better soon. I'll take my leave now. Thank you for your cooperation."

"I'll show you out," Catherine Deibert said. And she did, walking me quickly and stiffly to the door which she flung open as though to say, "Goodbye and good riddance."

"Thank you for your hospitality, ma'am," I told her with a tip of my cap as I went out.

The door slammed solidly behind me.

****

Frustrated, I drove back to town under a glowering gray sky. The wind hadn't let up. It whipped across the sere fields and tore leaves and branches from trees along the way. My roan paced at a good clip, as anxious to get to shelter as I was. I wrapped my scarf over my cap to cover my ears. Midway there it occurred to me to see where Runkle had been staying while in my town. There might be something there to connect him to Deibert.

****

"He pays on time, is quiet and keeps to himself," Matilda Rebuck said.

"Other than that, I don't know a thing about the man." She took the broom she'd been leaning on and proceeded to sweep the steps as though that ended the conversation.

"Does he have any visitors?" I asked, not ready to be put off just yet.

Tillie halted her sweeping, leaned on her broom again and scrutinized my face. "How'd you know he was stopping here?"

I gave her a cordial grin. "Why everybody knows you keep the best boarding house in town, Tillie."

"Yeah. So who told you?"

Tillie was an astute business woman. It was well known she had a couple girls in her employ did more than make the beds. Since her side-trade was discrete and drew no complaints from the public I was inclined to ignore it. But her suspicious nature didn't invite visits from the law. "Felix Buchner. Runkle has his rig at the livery."

Matilda nodded. "What's your interest in the man?"

"He got himself stabbed last night."

The startled look on Matilda's face told me it was a surprise to her. "It didn't happen here."

"No. I don't think it did. He was found on the highway, out on the other side of town."

"Maybe,' Tillie said, relief evident in the tone of her voice, "you should be inquiring at some of those drinking places over there then."

"I will be. Do you know, was he frequenting any of them?"

She shook her head. "Wasn't my business where he went or what he did when he wasn't here."

"Uh-huh. You still didn't answer my first question."

"Which was?"

"Did he have visitors?"

"None I'm aware of."

"What about your girls? Would they know anything?"

She gave me a squint-eyed look. "You'll have to ask them that."

"I intend to."

Her dark eyes raked me again. "Well, Elizabeth's inside. But I sent Barbara up to the store."

My stomach told me it was getting nigh onto noon and a glance at my pocket watch confirmed it. "Maybe I'll come back later. Got a few other things to tend to. I'll need to see Runkle's room, too, if you got no problem with that."

"Suit yourself," she said with a shrug and went back to her sweeping.

I started to walk away.

"Sheriff."

"Yes?" I turned back to face her.

"That man. Is he..."

"Dead? No. He was still holding his own this morning."

Matilda nodded. "Good. He seemed a decent sort. You might want to talk to Barbara. Seems they was cordial to one another."

****

Lydia scowled when I asked if she'd seen Barbara Frey.

Noting the look, I quickly explained my reason for seeking the girl. Lydia relaxed then and gave me a more welcoming smile. I love it when she smiles. My Lydia is a pretty girl and when she smiles her whole countenance glows in a way bound to make a person feel warm all over.

I should hasten to add, when I say "my Lydia" I mean it figuratively and not literally. Lydia Longlow is not a girl anyone can presume to own and I suspect her fierce independence is another reason she's turned down my ten or fifteen proposals of marriage to date. I haven't quite figured out what the other reasons might be since Lydia has told me she likes me and enjoys my company so long as it's on her terms.

Though I want to put a ring on her finger and stake my claim to a permanent relationship I consider myself fortunate to enjoy whatever dregs of affection I can secure on a regular basis.

Lydia is not only the prettiest girl I've ever known, she's also the smartest.

I stood there ogling her until she'd had enough of that nonsense and kicked me in the shin. "Is there something else you want, Sylvester," she said, her green eyes flashing, "or are you just going to stand there with your mouth hanging open? I do have other things to do, you know."

She was being truthful about that and I was rightly chastened. Lydia is one of the busiest women in Arahpot. Not only does she run the general store started by her father, she's also postmistress, head of the Women's Temperance League, a Sunday school teacher and sings in the Methodist church choir.

"I was hoping you might have time to make us a couple sandwiches and join me for lunch if you're not too busy," I told her.

Her full lips parted in another smile. "Since there's no one else in the store at the moment I guess I could manage that. Provided you don't mind if I sort today's mail while we eat. I have a fresh ham in back and I'll see what else I can find."

Basking in her benevolence, I sat on a cracker barrel and watched as she procured bread, sliced ham and Swiss cheese. She went forward to fish a couple pickles out of a brine cask. A beam of sunlight through the big front window tinted her auburn tresses with gold. Lydia is a big-boned girl, healthy-looking, who fills out her frocks in all the right places. She moves with the grace of a dancer and it pleasures me just to watch her. But when she cast a look in my direction and frowned I knew she'd had enough of my gawking. Anxious to avoid another scolding, I vacated my barrel and got us a couple sarsaparilla from the big double-door ice chest she'd installed last summer.

When I came back she had our lunch spread on the counter.

"So what have you been up to all morning besides stalking tarts?" she asked as I chomped down on a thick sandwich.

I told her what had transpired.

"That poor man," she said. "He was just in here yesterday afternoon."

"Runkle?"

"Who?"

"The man what was stabbed."

"Oh, no. I was talking about Mister Deibert. He came in with his wife and Reverend Huber. Poor man was almost doubled over with pain."

"Deibert?"

"Who else are we talking about?"

I nodded. "He claimed he felt poorly this morning, too. Did they come in for medicine?"

"No, silly," she said with a grimace. "I'm not a druggist. They wanted flypapers."

"Flypapers? At this time of year?"

"I thought it odd, too. Especially since she just got some the week before. But who am I to question what my customers want?" She paused to take a dainty bite of her sandwich, then sliced it in two and put the biggest piece on my plate. She went around to the far side of the counter and started separating letters behind the postal cage.

I'd finished my sandwich and gladly accepted her offering. After taking a mouthful, chewing and swallowing, I said, "Your new pastor seems to spend a lot of time in that couple's company." I'm not a regular churchgoer, though I was baptized in the same congregation. "He was out there this morning, too."

Lydia bobbed her head. "They seem very close."

"Yeah. Especially him and Mrs. Deibert. He couldn't keep his eyes off her the whole while I was there."

Lydia slapped the counter. "Sylvester! What a terrible thing to imply. He's a very decorous man. How could you think such a thing?"

I shrugged. "He's a man and a bachelor and Verbena's an attractive woman."

"Oh, an attractive woman. Perhaps it's you couldn't keep your eyes off her."

I chomped the last bit of pickle and wagged my head. "Now you know that's not the case. There's only one woman in Arahpot I have eyes for."

Though she tilted her head, it pleased me to see the smile my remark brought to her lips. I thought it best to quit while I was ahead.

CHAPTER 4

Runkle's eyes rolled back until I only saw the whites. Beads of perspiration glistened on the man's forehead and his skin looked gray and pasty. His breath gurgled and saliva mixed with foamy blood ran from his mouth. There was a sickly smell to the air, worse than I normally noticed in this room. I glanced at Doc.

"Fever's up," he said, using one hand to push me aside. He leaned close and dabbed a damp cloth across the man's face. "Don't think you're gonna get anything out of him for now."

It was disappointing. Simon had found me just as I was leaving Lydia's store. "Doc says you're to come right away if you want to talk to that man." We hurried back and I earned mean stares and even a couple vocal protests when I bustled past waiting patients and went right into Mariner's surgery. It was news I'd been hoping for but by the time we got back to Doc's place Runkle had relapsed again. "Did he tell you anything?"

Doc shook his head. "I sent Simon for you soon as I saw he was awake. I had questions to ask him but he did little save moan and grunt. It don't look good, Sylvester. Especially with this fever."

"His wounds that bad?"

Doc stood erect, facing me. "He was stabbed at least three times. One got him in the stomach. Not very deep and it doesn't appear to have struck any vital organs. He must have tried to grab the knife. There are cuts on the palm and fingers of his left hand. The second stab just grazed his ribs. No danger from that." He glanced back at his patient and I saw the worry in his eyes. "It's the third one that's bad. A lower chest wound is bad because it poses the risk of pneumothorax. It's like a leak in the lung. Not much I can do for him other than keep his wounds clean and packed. The fever's just another complication."

"You think he'll awake again?"

He shrugged. "It's in God's hands."

"Well that's not helping me, Doc, cause God's not telling me who done this and I'm not making a lot of progress on my own."

"I'm sorry. I wish there was more we both could do."

Embarrassed by my outburst, I put a hand on Mariner's shoulder. "I know. We're both frustrated. Can you at least tell me what kind of weapon I should be looking for?"

"Not exactly. It appears to have been a fairly big knife. Maybe a hunting knife. But, then, it could just as well have been a butcher knife."

In this community, neither one was going to narrow down my search.

****

"Is he gonna be okay?" Barbara Frey asked.

"Can't say for sure," I told her. "Doc's doing what he can."

We were seated around the table in Matilda Rebuck's kitchen—Elizabeth Kline and Barbara on one side, Matilda between us like a chaperone, and me. Tillie hadn't offered anything to eat or drink, but I didn't take offense. Lydia's lunch still provided ample sustenance.

Lizzie, a short, sullen-faced girl, promptly denied having any dealings with Runkle. "I've seen him about. That's all of it," she said.

Barbara, who is a pretty girl with frizzy blond hair, good skin and big blue eyes, freely admitted she'd changed the man's sheets and had talked to him a time or two. I didn't expect her to say she'd bedded with the man. That would have been too much to expect and wasn't my business anyway. Times were hard for young girls with no education. Tillie was a tight-fisted employer and I'm sure she took her share of any extra coin these girls earned on the side.

"What was the subject the time or two you talked?"

"Oh, you know," she said, licking a finger and running it across one eyebrow, "just the ordinary stuff strangers talk about. The weather, and where you come from and what you do." Those blue eyes explored me from head to waist as a smile flickered across her lips. It brought on a sweat under my clothes and I hoped my face wasn't as red as I thought it might be.

"And what did he tell you he did?"

"He said he had been a drummer but lately was working in a mercantile store in Lancaster." Barbara ran her pink tongue across her lips and gave me a friendly smile.

"Uh, and did he ever let on what he was doing up here?"

She waggled her head. "He did. Mister Runkle said there was a man owed him a big sum of money. It had taken him a long time to find where that man was hiding. But now he knew and he was going to get what was owed him."

"Did he tell you who this man was?"

She shook her head

I stood up. "Well, thank you, Barbara. Thank you, too, Lizzie. You've been a big help. Now, Tillie, you suppose I could have a look at Runkle's room and his belongings?"

"I suppose there's no harm in it," she said, rising, "you being the sheriff and all. His room wasn't paid beyond today. You think, if there's any money up there, I could..."

"I'll take his things along back to my office. Then you can go ahead and rent out the room if you want." I figured Tillie already knew if there was any money left in the room. I doubted I'd even be finding any.

"Oh," I said, turning back to Barbara, "did Mister Runkle ever mention if he had any family back in Lancaster? It'd be good if I could notify them."

"We never talked about that," Barbara said, following along behind Tillie and me.

****

Runkle wasn't a man for traveling heavy. He'd left a single portmanteau in the room, which was barely big enough for the single bed and small chest of drawers it held.

The small room had a funky stench. If Barbara had changed the bedding it hadn't been recently. As I threw the portmanteau up on the bed I noticed a pile of dirty stockings and a blue union suit in the corner next to the bureau. The obvious source of more fustiness.

Tillie and Barbara stood in the doorway, watching as I dumped out the contents of Runkle's bag. It didn't hold much. A change of clothes, more stockings, a bandana, a new pair of braces, comb, hairbrush, a can of mustache wax and a tin of *We Cure You* which, according to the label, was a sure therapy for the tobacco habit. I moved to the chest and started pulling out drawers. Only the top one held anything. More underclothes and socks. I stirred them around and felt something hard in one corner. A half-full box of .32 caliber Smith & Wesson cartridges. Strange. I hadn't come across a revolver. Nor had I found an overcoat. I'd have to ask Doc what Runkle was wearing when found. If he had a gun on him, why hadn't he defended himself?

As I pulled the cartridge box out of the drawer I noticed a wadded up paper jammed into the corner. It was an envelope sent to Runkle at a Lancaster address. The heading on the envelope read: Casey Detective Agency, Post Office Box 31, Harrisburg Pennsylvania. Under that in bold type was: *We Catch Those We Go After*

Unfortunately, the envelope was empty.

CHAPTER 5

My next stop that afternoon was the taverns in the area where Runkle was found. I hoped someone might have seen him or what happened. Even those who run honest establishments seem to have a reluctance to cooperate with the law. I've rousted drunks and ended brawls in all of them, so I wasn't optimistic about cooperation. It wasn't until the third and last on my list that I had a bit of luck.

"Yeah. I remember a fellow of that description was in here last night," Jake Beiler told me. "Only reason I recollect him was because of the girl."

"Girl? What girl?"

Beiler ran a rag across the bar in front of me. It did little to alter the stickiness of the surface and heightened the stink of stale beer which seemed to emanate from every nook and cranny of the place. His establishment, the *Bag o' Nails*, was only slightly more disreputable than the first two I'd visited that afternoon. He looked up at me now and grinned. "Pretty little thing. Don't know her name, but I've seen her around town before. Think she works in some boarding house."

That struck a chord and I was about to ask a question when he went on.

"Thought it was strange, girl like that comin' in here alone. But she went straight up to him like she was expected. She whispered somethin' in his ear which got him all agitated. He barked at her, seized her by the arm and they marched on out the door."

I leaned forward. "What was it he said to her?"

Beiler raised his shoulders and cocked his head. "Now how would I know that? They was at one end of the bar and I at the other. Couldn't hear what was said. It was just the raised voice drew my attention. I got to be on the alert for arguments that might lead to fights. I just saw what I told you. I figured they'd be back in a little while but they wasn't."

I squinted at the man. "What made you think they'd be back?"

"Why, 'cause he left his overcoat and it was a cold night, wasn't it? I figured they'd just gone outside to talk a moment where it was quieter. Thought he'd be back in shortly."

"And he wasn't?"

"Nah."

"The coat. Is it still here?"

Beiler frowned and nodded his head. "Sure. Told you I thought he'd be back. What? You think me or one of my customers would steal it? This isn't that kind of place. It's not a new coat, but it's a good one. When I saw it was getting late and he hadn't come back I put it here, under the counter, for safe-keeping. Figured the man would come back for a coat like this'n."

"You have it here now?"

"Sure I do."

"Let me see it then."

He drew the coat from under the bar and handed it over. It was one of those black Russia dog skin coats, quilted on the inside and with leather arm shields. A handsome fur coat, not new, a little frayed and stained in places, but not the kind of apparel a man would purposely leave behind. It felt a little heavy. Putting my hand in a pocket, I pulled out a .32 caliber Smith & Wesson hammerless revolver, fully loaded.

"Jeez," Beiler said with a snort, "didn't know that was in there."

"I'll be taking these things with me," I told him.

He cocked an eye at me. "You gonna return them to their owner? You'll tell him I kept them safe for him."

"They'll go where they're supposed to." I started for the door, then turned back. "The girl who was with him, would you recognize her if you saw her again?"

"Sure. Told you I'd seen her before. Just don't know her name."

As I went out, a tow-headed boy about eight or nine came round the side of the building, toting a slop jar looked to be heavier than him.

"Hey, boy, how come you're not in school?"

He gave me a sharp look and said, "'Cause it's a holiday."

"No holiday I heard about."

"Whyn't you mind your business, mister?" And he went on toward the twin privies standing in the backyard.

"What's your name, lad?"

"Nick," he hollered back. He sat down his bucket, flung open a privy door and stepped inside. Breeze carried the stench back to where I stood.

I gazed after him, then gave a shrug and moved on. I guessed he was right. It wasn't my business. If his parents didn't object to him missing out on free schooling who was I to care? I might have talked to Elmer Ritter, the newly appointed county truant officer. But I had other things to do.

Elated with the turn of events, I made for my rig, grateful for a breath of fresh air after the stink of Beiler's establishment. I hadn't expected much from my tavern tour but here I was, as excited as the day last year I got my new carriage. It's one of those extra-heavy mountain wagons advertised in the Sears, Roebuck and Company catalog. It cost me more than I could afford on my salary, but I'm real pleased with this rig come straight to me from the factory in Cincinnati, Ohio. The large seat with a full panel spring back is comfortable no matter how long my day gets. And these big wheels just plow right through the mud we get spring and fall.

Armed with my new ammunition, I drove straight back to Matilda Rebuck's place.

"I haint never—I didn't—it wasn't me went to that place," Barbara Frey said.

"You telling me you've never been to the *Bag o' Nails?*"

The girl's eyes skittered back and forth between me and Matilda. She hung her head and mumbled, "I might have been there sometime." Then she raised her head and looked directly at me. "But it warn't me last night."

"Maybe I should take you out there right now and let the proprietor tell me if you aren't the girl he saw talking to Mister Runkle."

The girl was scared. I could see it in the way her eyes couldn't hold steady on mine for long and heard it in the tremor of her voice. Matilda stood by the girl, her eyes locked on me, her mouth fixed in a straight line and one hand plucking at the stuff of her dress.

Matilda spoke up now, interceding in a way I hadn't expected. "It wasn't her. The girl was right here the whole night."

I swung on her. "You're tellin' me..."

Matilda took a step forward and stared me down. "Just what I said. She never put a foot out of here last night. Ask Lizzie. She'll tell you the same thing. The three of us sat in the kitchen drinking tea and playing cribbage from supper till time for bed."

The statement didn't please me and I spent a bit more time hemming and hawing. But the triumphant gleam in Matilda's eye told me she knew she had me. Much as I believed the pair of them were lying there was no way I could prove it. Even if I insisted on making good on my threat to take Barbara out to the *Bag o' Nails* I couldn't be certain Beiler would identify her. For the time being, they'd defeated me.

"I know you're lying," I said, looking right at Barbara. "I'll let you off for now. But I will be back. Meanwhile I want you to think on this, girl. A man is bad hurt. Maybe you had nothing to do with that. Whether you did or not, he's still hurt. You said he treated you kindly. You might be the only one in the whole wide world can help me bring whoever did this to justice. If you do know something and you don't help me, then you're not repaying his kindness. Just think on that, girl."

Barbara hung her head, not saying a word.

Disappointed, frustrated, I got back on my carriage and started back up town. Having failed in this, there was another task I could attend to.

We enjoy a lot of conveniences not available to past generations. Some of them, to my way of thinking, are mere flummery we could well do without. Others—such as advances in medicine and indoor plumbing—are God-sent. And there are a few which are downright blessings in the area of law enforcement.

One of these, for which I am mighty grateful, is the telegraph. This instrument by which we can communicate intelligence between several points at rapid speed is, in my humble opinion, a big improvement over sending messages by fast horse, homing pigeon or the railroad. Some are saying Mister Bell's telephone is going to replace it, but I don't see that happening. I mean, even if you can get the operator when you want her, you can't hardly hear the other party on local calls, let alone at any distance.

I'll stick by the telegraph, thank you.

It was my intention now to send a telegram to the detective agency in Harrisburg and see what it was they had to do with Runkle. But that intention was interrupted.

As I was coming down Market Street, Emma Mariner flagged me down.

"Thank goodness," she said, stepping down in the road next to my carriage, "we've been looking all over town for you."

CHAPTER 6

What had been an assault was now a murder.

"I sent Simon and the girls out looking for you right away," Doc told me. He looked awful peaked. I'd seen him look that way before when he'd lost a patient.

"I'm sure you did all you could for Runkle," I told him. "I'm sorry to hear about the man passing, but you didn't have to send the scouting party out to hunt me down. You could have sent Simon over to tell me when I came home."

Mariner sank onto a kitchen chair, embracing a mug of coffee in both hands. I was a little annoyed he hadn't offered me any. He pushed a chair out with one foot, inviting me to sit. Then he raised his eyes to meet mine. "Emma didn't tell you?" he asked.

"What?"

He shook his head. "I didn't have them looking for you to tell you the poor man had died." He blew on it, then took a sip of coffee while I waited for him to continue. "The man's wife has shown up."

"Here?"

He nodded. "In the parlor with Clara. Poor thing is distraught. Probably won't be able to talk to you for a while anyway."

I sat across from him, both hands on the table and leaning closer.

"How'd she know to come here?" I felt tired myself. It had been a long day. I'd come directly over to Mariner's after unhitching and stabling my horse and tending to its needs. I sighed knowing tomorrow I'll have to get together with Squire Charlie Fegley and empanel a jury for an inquest. It won't be a big problem since Doc is both the coroner and chief witness. Still it's another task falling in my already busy lap. I haven't had a deputy since young Booth Wilkins took it in his head to join the army and go fight Indians in Texas or some other God-forsaken place instead of staying here where it's generally safe and reasonably civilized.

"She had his address. Matilda told her what had happened and she came right over." He took another drink of coffee. "It was too late."

I frowned. Tillie hadn't told me that either. But then I hadn't learned anything else I wanted to know at the boarding house.

Emma came in and stood by the stove. "Would you like a cup of coffee, Sylvester?"

"Sure would," I said, grateful.

"Why didn't you tell Sylvester about Mrs. Runkle?" her father asked as Emma brought my coffee.

"I thought you'd want to do that yourself."

I poured cream in my cup and then stirred in a couple spoons of sugar, wondering how much the woman might know about why her husband came to our town and what he was up to with the detectives.

"Mother said to invite you for supper, Sylvester—unless you were going to Lydia's," Emma said.

Lydia hadn't invited me and I figured anything I got in this house would be superior to what I might get up for myself. "I'd be pleased to stay," I said, and I saw the response pleased Emma.

Hiram said Clara had insisted Mrs. Runkle stay with them as long as need be. I could have offered her a room at my house, too. There are plenty of empty rooms. Still it probably wouldn't have been proper, me being a bachelor.

"Good idea," Doc said. "Maybe the woman will be fit to talk to you afterwards."

****

Mrs. Runkle agreed to talk to me after supper. We might as well have done it right away since no one—including me—ate much after seeing how upset the woman was over her husband's death. Clara had roasted a chicken and prepared all the usual fixings. I thought it a waste to ignore so much good food but felt better about it when Sissy suggested maybe everybody would feel up to eating the chicken cold later on.

"You can use my study, if you like," Hiram said.

"You want to set in?"

"You don't mind?"

"Maybe between the two of us we can think of questions one of us might overlook."

"Can I come, too?" Simon asked.

"No you may not," Doc said, placing a hand on the lad's head. "This is not a situation for children. Besides, you have school work to occupy you before bedtime." He dismissed the boy with a wave of one hand.

Then he led us down the hall.

Hiram seated Mrs. Runkle on a Morris chair by the door, motioned for me to take his desk chair and sat himself down on a chest by the opposite wall. Mrs. Runkle pulled a handkerchief from her sleeve, dabbed at both eyes and said, "I'm ready, Sheriff."

She was a tiny woman, barely five foot tall and couldn't have weighed more than a hundred pounds. The woman had frizzy gray hair and her brown eyes looked twice as large as they were behind thick-lensed spectacles. She looked older than her husband, but I suppose that's the lot of most married women who seem to experience more age-wearing trials than we men. Lydia's always telling me how much easier life is for men.

Mrs. Runkle snuffled once more, then asked, "Where should I start?"

"The beginning's always a good place," I said. "Do you know what your husband was doing here?"

She sighed and glanced from Doc to me. "I believe he came here to kill a man," she said in a strained voice.

That brought my head up in a hurry and I heard Hiram snort.

"Oh, I don't want you to misunderstand. My husband was a good man. A moral man. But he believed this man had ruined our lives and he intended to punish him. That's why, as soon as I'd found out where he'd gone, I came after him. I wanted to stop him. To tell him it didn't matter, that we should just get on with our lives."

"What had this man done?" Mariner asked.

"My husband had been a respectable businessman in Lancaster County. He had a thriving mercantile establishment. Like many men who have worked themselves up from poverty, he had a little streak of avarice in him. Oh, I don't mean that in a bad way. I mean, he had worked so hard for what he'd got, he constantly craved for more security."

Mariner started to rise. "Would you like something to drink, Mrs. Runkle? I could have my wife bring us some tea. Or wine, if you prefer."

The woman raised a deprecating hand. "No. I'm fine. I think I'll feel better getting this all off my chest."

Hiram sat back down. I spun around in his chair, relishing what a comfortable seat it was. "Go on, Mrs. Runkle."

"Well, we never had any children. It was just the two of us and I was plenty satisfied with what we had. But this man—this devil—he came along and tempted Conrad, made him think he could make him truly rich."

"Can you identify this man?" I blurted.

She shook her head and I saw the moisture well in her eyes again. She pulled off her glasses, dropped them in her lap and dabbed at her eyes. "I never saw him. Conrad always said there was no need for women to involve themselves in a man's business. He said he would take care of me. And he always did to my satisfaction. Up until this time.

"This man, this evil man, he sucked all the sustenance out of my husband's business in less than a year's time. I don't really understand how it happened. But, suddenly, the man was gone and my husband was declaring bankruptcy." The poor woman commenced to sob. We were so stricken at the sight, both Hiram and I rose and patted the woman on her shoulders. We didn't know what else to do.

That was when Clara came in and made us stop. "Can't you see, the woman is distraught enough," she barked at Hiram and gave me a scathing look as well. "I'm putting her to bed now. You can resume your interview in the morning."

OCTOBER 6, 1897

CHAPTER 7

I was up earlier than usual the next morning, eager to hear the rest of Mrs. Runkle's tale. After a hasty breakfast, I passed a half hour or two biting my nails and peering out the front curtains looking for sign the Mariners were up and ready for a visitor. Finally I saw Simon come out the side door to dump a pan of stove-ash. I grabbed my coat and cap off the rack and put them on.

I was halfway across my lawn when I encountered Lydia coming down from her place on Seventh Street. In good weather she often walks from her house to the store down on Market Street. It's only a block and a half away.

"Good morning, Syl." She greeted me with a bright smile.

I stopped and took stock of her. Clad in a blue cashmere Mackintosh with pearl buttons and a velvet collar, she came striding toward me, her outfit topped with a jaunty Cambridge hat with a ribbon band. I stared, on any day she was a sight to behold.

"How'd you know I'd be passing?" she asked, stopping in front of me. "Were you watching for me?"

What could I do but nod assent?

"Will you walk me to work then? I doubt there are any about this early, but no rowdy is likely to accost me with you as escort."

With an anxious glance toward Mariner's, I offered her my arm. I count it a privilege any moment I can spend in Lydia's company. Despite my curiosity about Runkle, I knew this delay would provide time for the family to eat their breakfast and for Mrs. Runkle's nerves to settle down.

"I see you didn't starve to death last night," Lydia said as we walked along. "I would have fed you, but I had choir practice and I figured you could fend for yourself one night."

"I ate with the Mariners."

"Again?"

"It was business." I explained about Mrs. Runkle.

"Anyway, I'll bet it was Emma invited you."

"She did," I conceded.

"See. The girl has her cap set for you. Maybe you should marry Emma."

"It's not Emma I'm in love with."

I thought my remark brought a blush to her cheek, but it could have been nothing more than the chill in the air.

We were approaching the store when Lydia said, "I think that girl has an interest in you, too."

When I looked in the direction she indicated, I saw Barbara Frey scurrying away around the corner. "I think she'd prefer to avoid me," I said.

****

"The man made us poor," Mrs. Runkle said. "That was difficult for my husband to abide. I tried to convince him it wasn't important. We'd been poor before and I assured him we could survive. But it was too great a burden for him. His despair wouldn't allow him to focus on anything else. It drove a wedge between us and I left him." She looked at me and I saw shame in her expression. "A wife is supposed to support her husband no matter what. I was weak. I just couldn't take it any more. Maybe if I'd stayed with him..."

I reached out and patted her hand. "What happened wasn't your fault, Mrs. Runkle. Your husband should have gone to the police. He shouldn't have tried to bring this man to justice on his own."

"Oh, but he did," she told me. "He was embarrassed at first. I mean, he prided himself on being a smart businessman. It was difficult for him to admit this man had got the better of him. But when he learned we weren't the only ones cheated Conrad went to the police and gave evidence.

"The man was too slippery. The police weren't able to find him. Time went on and there were no results. My husband got more and more desperate. All he could think about was catching this man and making him pay. That's when I left him. I thought it might bring him to his senses. If he valued our relationship, he might give up his desire for revenge."

"Would you like more tea, Mrs. Runkle?"

"Maybe a half-cup."

We were alone in the Mariner kitchen. Hiram was seeing patients and Clara had provided us with a fresh pot of Gunpowder-Moyune and a fresh-baked shoofly pie. Now I'm not much of a tea drinker but this stuff wasn't bad. It went well with the pie and I was having my second cup. I topped off hers and sat back down.

"How did you know your husband had come up here?"

She took time for a sip of tea before replying. "He confided in a friend that he was in pursuit of the fiend. Later he wrote a letter to this friend and enclosed the address of the boarding house where he was staying. The friend grew concerned because Conrad said he wanted someone to know where he'd gone in case things went wrong. That's when his confidant contacted me."

"Did you know your husband had engaged a detective agency?"

She gave me a surprised look. "No. I had no idea."

"I found an envelope. The letter was missing. But perhaps that's how he knew his quarry was here." Leaning across the table, I took her hand in mine and asked, "Do you know the name of the man your husband was tracking?"

"He was called Phoebus Potteiger."

The name didn't mean a blamed thing to me.

****

The hardest part of the inquest was getting it organized. Right after talking to Mrs. Runkle I got together with Squire Fegley. Charlie drew up a list of six reputable men for the jury (with a few substitutes in case any he named were indisposed) and sent me off to recruit them. That had me running all over the countryside for the next hour and wishing I still had a deputy who might have handled this for me.

Some might think it easy to find a deputy in a town this size. Admittedly the job isn't that hard. Most times it's just plain boring with little more to do than serve papers and sit around the office waiting for someone to break the law. We're a pretty quiet community. Over in Shannon and in some of our other mining patches where there's a foreign mix that don't get along with one another a lawman can be kept busy. Here we're mostly the same breed of native-born Americans and get along fairly well, except when liquor or gambling and such get people out of sorts. The main problem is the job doesn't pay much. Aside from those who are farming, the railroad gets our best men and pays a lot more than the town can afford. And, as a few have told me, the job might be easy but there's still always the chance a man could get shot.

So I go along day by day, doing the best I can by myself, hoping eventually I will get another deputy. Simon helps me out from time to time, running errands. He says he'll be my deputy once he's old enough. I hope I don't have to wait that long. The child is only eleven.

While I was in town rounding up the jurymen I stopped by the telegraph office and sent off a message to the detective agency, explaining what had happened and asking what was in the letter they'd sent Runkle. The sooner I had that, I figured, I'd have more of a clue as to where to find this Phoebus Potteiger.

There were still other things puzzling me. Like why Valentine Deibert looked so scared on seeing Runkle. I didn't believe the man had simply been startled over being bumped into. That didn't make any sense. And then there was Barbara Frey. That girl needed more leaning on, too.

****

Once I had them gathered, Charlie impaneled the jury consisting of James L. Baker, foreman; William Dunn, Christopher Shipman, Thomas Betz, Ira Ritter and Nicholas Strickland.

We trudged on out to where Runkle had been found. There wasn't a blamed thing to be seen there. But the rules said the jury had to visit the scene of the crime. Ollie Cramer, the teamster, was the first witness and explained how he had come to find Runkle lying on the road. Hiram Mariner, speaking as witness, told how the victim was delivered to him.

Because of her distraught condition, Doc spoke on behalf of the widow. I, then, did my part. I left out my conversations with the Deiberts, Beiler and Barbara Frey. No use bringing speculation into the picture at this early juncture.

Since there weren't any other witnesses to be called, Doc Mariner took the floor as coroner and described the victim's injuries and his death.

After that we (Doc, me and the squire) went back to Charlie's office and had a cup of coffee while the jury convened in the backroom of Baker's hardware store next door. We hadn't even finished the first cup before they were back with their verdict.

"We found that the said Conrad Runkle came to his death from a stab wound to his lower chest, inflicted by the hand or hands of some person or persons unknown," Baker told us in a solemn tone.

Naturally it wasn't a verdict we didn't expect.

"Well then," Charlie Fegley said, turning to me, "I've already spoke to the district attorney over to Shannon. He said, since his people are already busy with a number of other crimes, he's satisfied to let you carry on with the observations you've already begun. You can keep him informed through me. That all right with you, Syl?"

I told him I had no objections.

****

Plucking out my pocket watch, I saw it was well past noon. My stomach was already telling me that. I climbed aboard my carriage and headed up Market Street. I figured as I was in the neighborhood I'd stop by the store and see what Lydia had available for lunch. After that I thought I'd have a go at seeing if I could break Barbara Frey's fabrication or at least make her more nervous. Keep the mental pressure on a person long enough and it'll have them telling the tale you want to hear quicker than any physical pain you might inflict.

Another minute or two and I got a stab of pain I wasn't expecting.

Just as I rode down the hill which levels out in front of the store I saw Lydia come out the door. I was about to call to her when a man followed. At first I figured him for a customer. She turned and locked the door. Then the man held out his arm to her and the two of them went strutting up the street, chattering away like a courting couple. I was too far away to get a good look at his features. But he was a tall fellow, about our age, wearing a square crown hat at a rakish angle. He had on a black overcoat and walked with a swagger that dared any to challenge his right to escort my girl.

As I watched them disappear up the road my hunger was replaced with a chunk of cast iron in my gut.

CHAPTER 8

"You don't need to be nasty, Sylvester Tilghman."

I didn't, but my hurt over seeing Lydia with another man made me more unkind to Barbara Frey than I'd intended. "If you'll answer my questions maybe I'll ease off on you," I told her.

I'd found the girl hanging wash in the side-yard of Matilda's establishment and pounced on her like a fox on a chick.

Barbara pouted and plunked herself down on a bench. She stuck her tongue out at me and drew cigarette fixings from the pocket of her skirt. The girl busied herself rolling a smoke but I saw her hands shaking and her eyes were moist.

"You going to smoke that thing?"

She glanced up at me. "Why the hell else would I make it?"

I wasn't used to seeing a girl smoking. I'd never got the habit and didn't admire it in men. With women I thought it was just downright undignified. "Doc says those things haint healthy."

"Phooey on Doc." She struck a match, lit the cigarette and took a drag. That quick she started to hack and snort. She was bent over, turning red in the face. I stepped up and clapped her on the back a couple times. She stopped sputtering, sat up and ground out the cigarette on the side of the bench.

"You ever smoke one of those things before?"

She shook her head. "Never. The fixings belong to Lizzie."

"Then why'd you try it now?"

"Cause you're making me nervous with all your questions. I didn't do nothing wrong."

I sat down beside her. It was a tight fit on the bench and I thought she'd scoot over, but she didn't. "I think you did, Barbara. You went out to the *Bag* and whispered in Runkle's ear. He left the place with you and he didn't come back. Were you the one stabbed him?"

She jerked around facing me. "I never hurt him. He was always nice to me." A tear rolled from the corner of one eye and coursed over her cheek.

"Then you admit you were out there?"

"No! I never said that." She wiggled closer, pushing her thigh against mine.

"Tell you what," I said, feeling generous, "Why don't you come with me out to the tavern right now? Let my witness have a look at you. If he says it wasn't you I won't bother you no more."

Barbara laid a hand on my leg and gave me what I can only describe as a lascivious look. "I've got a better idea, Syl. Why don't we go upstairs to my room? I won't ask a penny if you'll promise to leave me out of this."

I jerked away from her and stood up. "You know I can't do nothing like that."

"Why not? Other men..."

"I'm not other men. I'm the sheriff and I'm investigating a murder. If you don't soon cooperate I'm going to start seriously considering you were the person who stabbed poor Conrad Runkle to death—which I haven't up to this point. I think you do know more than you're telling me. And I'm going to keep right on pressuring you until you tell me the truth."

Barbara sighed and hung her head and I could see more tears dropping off her face and wetting her dress. I sat down beside her again, a new tactic having entered my brain. "You say you and Lizzie and Matilda were playing cribbage that night?"

She glanced up at me, swiping the back of her hand across her eyes.

"That's right. I told you that and so did Tillie."

"Which version were you playing?"

"Huh?" She looked at me, puzzled.

"Which version?"

"Why, just regular old cribbage. You know, the card game."

"Yes, but there are different varieties of the game. You can play with five, six or eight cards to a person. Which did you play?"

"I guess it must have been six," she said after a moment's thought.

"Uh-huh."

Just then the side door popped open and Matilda stuck her head out. "What's goin' on here?"

"Sylvester's been pestering me again about the other night."

"I was just asking her about your cribbage game."

"What about it?"

"I asked how many cards was dealt?"

"Why everybody knows you play with five cards each."

"Barbara said six."

Tillie glanced at the girl, then back at me with a scowl. "She's mistaken. Girl never could count any better than she can spell."

"So how many people were playing?"

Matilda stepped out in the yard and gave me an icy glare. "Already told you—her, me and Lizzie. What're you trying to say here?"

"That's three people. You can't play cribbage with three people. It's a game for two or four players." There is actually one version which allows three players, but I was hoping they weren't aware of it.

"Why we must have been taking turns then," Matilda said.

"Oh, stop!" Barbara cried, jumping up and throwing her hands over her face. "I know you want to protect me, Tillie. But it's no use. He just won't give up." She spun around and faced me. "I'll tell you what you want to know. I was there. But I sure didn't kill him."

****

Maybe it was a mistake. Sometimes it's hard to know in hindsight how things might have turned out if you'd done this or that. Barbara was so wrought up I agreed to give her till the morning to tell me what had transpired the night Runkle was killed. The girl promised me she wouldn't run away and Tillie gave her assurance I'd have my answers first thing in the morning. It was getting late, I was hungry and I had their word I'd soon know what I wanted. Maybe I was a fool.

I went on home, plodding up to the door contemplating what might be available inside to make up for the lunch I'd missed. There was a note pinned to the screen door. Soon as I plucked it off I recognized Lydia's distinctive script.

Sylvester, it read, *come over to the house for supper. There's someone I want you to meet. Yours, Lydia.*

That stone plonked in my gut again. Well, if she wanted to introduce me to her new beau I figured I might as well get it over with. At least I would be assured of a good meal, providing I was up to eating it.

Her father must have been watching for me. He opened the door at my first knock and greeted me friendly as always. I respected the way Lydia cared for her elderly parents and I genuinely liked the old couple. I had a staunch ally in Mister Longlow. He sympathized with my goal and often said he was puzzled at Lydia's reluctance to become my bride. "She'll be an old maid before long," he'd told me just last week. "I can't understand why the girl won't accept your proposal. She won't get a better offer."

I was grateful for his support, but after what I'd seen earlier this day I had a sour outlook as to what lay ahead.

"Sylvester," the old man said now, ushering me in. "We've been waiting for you. Let me take your coat. Everybody's in the parlor. Go right on in." I shucked my coat and gave it and my cap to him. I heard the piano through the closed parlor door and Lydia's sweet voice raised in song. As I opened the door and prepared to step through, Lydia was joined by a strong tenor in the chorus of *After the Ball*. What an appropriate song, I thought. I figured my dance was about done.

Lydia's mother sat in her rocker, rapt by the music. My sweetheart turned her head and ceased playing as she saw me. The tenor went on another bar, then stopped dead and also turned to face me. He had a longish shock of blond hair, a ruddy complexion and a bushy mustache. He wore a natty blue suit with striped trousers.

"Syl," Lydia said, rising and greeting me with a bounteous smile. "You got my note. Good. Supper's all ready. We've just been enjoying some music while we waited for you."

I crossed toward her slowly, accepting a friendly nod from her mother en route.

"I want you to meet somebody," Lydia said, taking the stranger's arm and leading him toward me.

My stomach twisted in knots.

"This is Cyrus Gutshall," Lydia said. "My very dear cousin."

Cousin? I paused.

"I've heard a lot about you, sport," Gutshall said, extending a hand.

I gave him my hand and he squeezed it in a firm grip. "I-I..." I stammered.

"Cyrus is just back from the wild west," Lydia exclaimed. "He has so many wonderful stories to tell. I've already heard some. But I won't mind a bit if he repeats them for you."

I met his steady stare. "You're not from around here."

"I grew up in Shannon. Couldn't stand the thought of working in the mines like my dad. So I joined the army as soon as I was of age."

"Knew another fellow did that recently," I said, thinking of my former deputy.

****

Gutshall soon proved himself to be a braggart and a know-it-all. I didn't care. So long as he wasn't replacing me in Lydia's affections I was content to let him blow all he wanted. Since she and her parents seemed to regard him as some sort of gift from Heaven I was also willing to pretend I was equally fascinated by the man and his tales—ninety percent of which I believed were pure fabrications.

As usual, Lydia's cooking was of a quality to make me forget my troubles and forgive any transgressions which might have marred the day. We had us a nice supper of oyster stew, beef with vegetables, boiled potatoes and stewed tomatoes, with pumpkin pie for dessert. How the girl found time to do all this after working a full day in the store and visiting with her cousin was beyond me. True she had some help from her mother, but Mrs. Longlow had slowed considerably in recent years and the old man had confided in me long ago his wife never did have the culinary skills of their daughter.

Filled to capacity, we retired to the parlor after supper and Gutshall regaled us with more of his tall-tales while the women did up the dishes. Actually it was mostly me had to listen to the stories. Mister Longlow nodded and snored until the women returned and his wife smacked him awake. The evening concluded after more piano-playing by Lydia and songs from her and her cousin.

I went home a happy man, my belly full and confident I was still basking in Lydia's affections even if she wasn't willing to marry me. My sleep was deep and untroubled by thought of Runkle's murder and what lay before me on the morrow.

OCTOBER 7, 1897

CHAPTER 9

I followed a hearse out the road without thinking much about it. People died every day and it wasn't unusual to see Undertaker Follmer going about his business. But when his rig turned into the same lane I was headed for I gigged up my horse.

"What're you doing here, Virgil?" I called pulling up alongside his rig in front of the house.

"Well what do you think, Sheriff? I'm here to pick up a body. Did they call for you, too?" Follmer reined in and his assistant Floyd jumped down and tied up at the hitching post.

As I alighted I noticed Doc Mariner's buggy at the side of the house. What in blazes was going on? Follmer joined me and we went up on the porch while Floyd stayed with the hearse. Follmer knocked and Catherine Deibert promptly opened the door and ushered us in. I was even more puzzled to see that hard-faced woman all teary-eyed, sniffling and dabbing at her red nose with a hanky.

"In here," she said, ushering us into the same parlor where I'd met with the family previously.

There we found Hiram Mariner administering to Mrs. Deibert who was stretched out on the sofa. He passed a little vial back and forth under her nose while Preacher Huber knelt beside them, patting her hand. In a moment or two, the woman sputtered and tried to sit up but Doc restrained her. "Just lie still and catch your breath," he told her. "You'll be all right."

"What's going on here, Hiram?" I asked, striding over to them.

Reverend Huber glanced up at me. "Mister Deibert has passed away."

"What? When did this happen?"

Hiram rose and took my arm. "Over night. Come on over here and I'll fill you in. Look after Mrs. Deibert, will you Reverend." He escorted me across the room, out of earshot of the others.

"I didn't realize the man was so sick," I said.

Doc cast a look back at the new widow who was now being cooed at by her pastor. Catherine Deibert was in conference beyond them with Virgil Follmer. "It doesn't appear to have been a natural death," Hiram told me.

"I think me and you need to talk."

He nodded. "We will. But right now I got to get together with Virgil and make sure the body goes to my surgery. I need to do an autopsy before he goes destroying evidence with his process. Come to the house after you're done here." He started back across the room, then stopped and looked back at me. "What are you doing here anyway? Did somebody send for you?"

"That's another story. We'll get together later. Is the widow up to talking to me?"

"Give her a few minutes. She was the one found the body. I guess it came as a shock."

****

"He ate a hearty supper last night," Verbena Deibert said. "He seemed much improved over the past few days. I don't know what could have happened." She passed a perfumed handkerchief under her nose and I was seated close enough to catch a whiff of the sharp scent though I couldn't have distinguished it from a dozen others. Verbena was clad in a blue polka-dot flannelette wrapper. Despite her ordeal and frequent employment of the anti-fainting scent, she looked fresh and pretty enough for an outing.

Though I would have preferred interviewing her alone, Reverend Huber insisted on sitting on one side of her while Catherine Deibert squeezed onto the other on the sofa. Seated on a big hassock, I faced the trio. I supposed the arrangement was just as well since I could then question all of them at once.

"He did seem better," Catherine said. "He asked me to make salt mackerel for his breakfast. He was partial to the dish when his stomach was up to it."

"We played dominoes last night and he seemed in fine temper," Huber added.

"You spent the night here, Reverend?"

"I was invited."

"It was late," Catherine explained. "It would have been senseless for him to go when we have plenty of room here."

"Especially when I was coming back again in the morning."

"Oh?"

"For my lessons," Verbena put in. "Valentine said Leonard might as well join us for breakfast since he also likes mackerel."

"Makes sense I guess," I said, nodding my head.

"Why did you come this morning, Sheriff?" Catherine asked, squinting at me. "Did you intend insulting my brother again with that nonsense about that poor man who was stabbed?"

"Actually my interest was in seeing you, Mrs. Deibert."

"Me?" Verbena asked, raising a dainty hand to her face.

"I've been informed you sent Barbara Frey to give a message to Runkle the night he was attacked. Barbara says you wanted him to come outside the *Bag O' Nails* to talk with you."

"I never..." she started, flushing.

"Who is this Frey person?" Catherine demanded.

"She's one of the girls works at Matilda Rebuck's boarding house."

"Those trollops," the preacher said, rolling his eyes. "You would believe one of them over Mrs. Deibert?"

"Now that's not a very Christian attitude, Reverend."

"Maybe not, but those girls do have a reputation around town."

"That may be so, but gossip often counts more toward reputation than fact. The girl told me something and I'm just asking Mrs. Deibert to comment on it. I haven't said anything about believing anybody yet."

"Well," Verbena said, her voice taking on a haughty tone, "you might consider the source. I don't know why this girl is telling you such an absurd tale. I don't know her and I didn't know this Runkle person either. Why would I want to talk to a man I didn't know?"

"Are you accusing Mrs. Deibert of killing this fellow?" Huber asked.

I put my hands together and cracked my knuckles, earning a grimace and a grunt from Catherine. "Not at this point," I told the preacher. Then I cocked an eye at the Widow Deibert. "You say you didn't know the man. Unless I ask, I have no way of knowing that. You might have known him before you moved here."

She stared at me, gathering her thoughts. It was quiet enough in the room for me to hear the sibilance of her breathing and the tick of a clock close by in another room. "I didn't know the man," Verbena said, finally. "He was—what? Did you say some sort of drummer?"

"I never did say."

Above us we heard a muffled drone of voices and movement as Follmer and his man prepared to move the body. A little while and they came clomping down the stairs and along the hall. A door slammed. Catherine shuddered. I looked but saw no sign of emotions from the other two.

"Well, I must have heard it somewhere," Verbena said and passed the smelling scent under her nose again.

"Look here, Sheriff," the pastor said, rising and looking down on me. "I think Mrs. Deibert has had about enough for the time being. Will you have a little compassion and continue this another time?"

I stood up. I was taller than him by nearly a head. It was my turn to look down on him. "I can do that," I said. "My condolences on your loss, ladies. I'll show myself out." I started for the door, then turned back suddenly. "But, I need to warn you, Mrs. Deibert. We will be talking again."

****

"Arsenic," Doc said.

I gaped at him. "Two murders in a couple days. What's happening to our quiet town?"

Mariner raised a hand. "I don't intend to mislead you, Syl. I said it appears not to have been a natural death and I believe I'm right about that."

I stared down at the body on the table between us, then back at Hiram. "I don't understand. How could it be an unnatural death and not a case of murder?" Not really intending to, I glanced down at Valentine Deibert's corpse again. A sheet covered him up to his shoulders. His flabby white face was waxen and I was glad the eyes were closed.

"It was arsenic killed him," Hiram explained. "I don't have to open him up to tell that. Here, I'll show you." He pulled back the sheet, exposing one of Deibert's hands. He took it in his and turned it over. The flesh was red and rough, dotted with black spots. "See that? And look at the fingernails," he added, turning the hand again. "Those are all signs of arsenic poisoning. Long-term. I'll run some tests, but I'm ninety-nine percent sure that's what killed him."

"Then it must have been murder."

Hiram shook his head. "Not necessarily. It could have been accidental, or intentional."

"You mean suicide?" I thought about how frightened the man had appeared that day in the store.

"That's certainly a possibility. But I think it less likely than the other."

"Then it could be murder?"

He nodded. "Or simply an unfortunate accident."

"Was Deibert your patient?"

"He came to me when they first moved here. He didn't like my diagnosis. I told him most of his alleged ailments were figments of his imagination, what he needed was to eat less and move more."

"I don't suppose he liked hearing that."

"No. He didn't. He stopped coming to me. I heard he started visiting Ollie Kintzler."

"The pow-wow doctor."

Hiram nodded. "It's surprising in this day and age how many people still put stock in such superstition."

"Some say it gets results." I'd seen too many things I couldn't explain to totally write off the hexerei. But I wasn't going to confess that to Mariner. "Do you think the arsenic came from him?"

The doctor shrugged. "I don't know. I do know Walt Hockenbroch, the pharmacist, told me Deibert bought every kind of potion and notion he could. The man was addicted to self-medication. Some of those elixirs contain arsenic."

"So you're saying the man could have imbibed..."

"Enough to kill him? It's too early for me to say. You and I, my friend, have more work ahead before we can decide if this was murder, suicide or an accident."

CHAPTER 10

On the days when I'm not busy—which used to be most days—I like to walk down to the railroad station in the late afternoon and watch the passenger train come in. I see people arriving and departing and I flex my mind, wondering about their lives, their peregrinations, their eventual destinies. Sometimes when I'm particularly dispirited, those times when Lydia has once again turned down my proposal, I consider what might be my destiny should I board the train and take off for nether regions.

Of course I could never do that. How could I leave Arahpot when there's still the possibility Lydia might concede to my petition some day?

As I walked down Market Street toward my office I was pining for a sight of her, since I hadn't seen her all day. After leaving Mariner's I had to go once more to Charlie Fegley's to inform the justice about Deibert's death. We'd be impaneling another jury once Doc was done with his autopsy. Meanwhile Charlie and I drew up a list of potential jurors and then I went around to inform each of them of the need to be available when called.

It was getting nigh onto lunch time now and I still had a full day of duties ahead of me. I stopped by the butcher shop and bought a link of summer sausage. Ours isn't as good as the bologna they make down in

Lebanon County but it would have to do. I didn't have time for a real sit-down lunch. I got some rolls from the bakery next door and went in my office, intending to heat up what was left of a pot of coffee while I ate. The office was damp. I fed my stove, set the pot to warm and settled down at my desk to eat. Just as I gnawed off the first bite, the office door popped open.

"There you are," Cyrus Gutshall said, coming in uninvited. "I came by earlier and you weren't here. So I thought I'd try again."

I chomped my sandwich, unable to reply with a full mouth.

"Lydia thought you and I should have some time together, old sport," he blathered on, "and I think it might be a good idea, too. Us both being adventurous men, I expect we have plenty in common and lots to talk about. How long have you been sheriff?"

I managed to swallow my meat, nearly choking in the process.

"Say, that sausage looks mighty good," Gutshall said, leaning across my desk and leaning so close I smelled his tonic water. "You couldn't spare a bit, could you? I haven't had lunch today."

"I don't really have time to chat, Cyrus," I told him, leaning back in my chair. "I'm really busy."

Without awaiting permission, he tore off a piece of my meat. "This really looks nice. I don't mind tagging along if it's okay with you. I promise not to get in the way. I'd just like to see how you manage your day." He smiled and brushed at his big mustache, then bit into the sausage. "Got any coffee?" he muttered.

At that point I was wishing those wild Indians had got him while he was out west. Since they hadn't I figured I was stuck with the man until I could either bore him or find some other means of dissuading him from tracking along with me.

Gutshall finished off most of my meat, the last roll and half the coffee (which he complained was the worst he'd ever drank). "So, where we going first, chief?" he asked.

An idea dawned on me. I didn't really have to be present, but I thought it might get him off my tail. "I have to attend an autopsy."

"Great. That sounds interesting. I've never seen one. Is it a murder case?"

"This is to determine the cause of death. They aren't a pleasant thing to watch. Lots of blood and such. You sure you want to come along?"

Gutshall chuckled. "Sounds like fun. I'm not a bit squeamish."

And he wasn't. Doc said afterward I did more blanching than Gutshall, and it wasn't my first time attending an autopsy. The cause of Deibert's death—as expected—was arsenic poisoning.

"So, what's our next stop?" Gutshall asked as we headed outside.

I had some other stops in mind—Barbara Frey, Mrs. Deibert, Walt Hockenbroch and old Kintzler—but I didn't want Gutshall tagging along. "I've got to get back to the office and write up a report. Then I'll take it over to the squire and we'll put our heads together and decide what time to hold the inquest tomorrow."

He frowned. "Oh, that sounds rather boring, old champ." He pulled out an expensive-looking pocket-watch on a gold chain, flipped it open and checked the time. "I do have some errands to run. Maybe I'll join up with you another time."

I breathed a sigh of relief as he started to walk away.

Then he spun around. "Say, I almost forgot. Lydia said she has choir practice again tonight and won't be able to feed us. What do you say you come on down to the hotel and I'll buy you supper? Afterward maybe we can play a couple hands of poker."

"No," I said, shaking my head. "I have lots of paperwork to catch up on. By the time I get done with that I'll be ready for bed."

"All right. Maybe another time. Lydia told me you're in the market for a new deputy. Maybe if the job proves interesting enough I might consider it."

I'm sure I paled, but I don't know if he noticed.

****

"Just the man I wanted to see," James Baker said, bustling into my office just as I was about to leave. "You've got to arrest that man."

"Who?"

"Why that doctor. Who the blazes you think I'm talking about?"

"Doc Mariner?"

Baker scowled. "No. Not *our* doctor. I'm talking about that medicine show fakir who's been selling his wares all week down on the corner. The man is a cheat and I want him arrested."

I'd seen the man, but with everything else going on hadn't paid him much attention. I was supposed to see that people like him and drummers and such were licensed by the town. I hadn't had time and, not having had any complaints before this, let it slide. "What's he done that's criminal?" I asked.

"Why he's taking people's money under false pretenses, that's what. Here, look at this." Baker thrust a little papier-mâché box at me. I lifted the lid and peered at it. "Looks like sawdust," I told him.

"Exactly. That's just what it is."

"The man's selling sawdust?"

Baker nodded. "Passing it off as a cure-all," he said, sneering. "He's cheating foolish people out of their money."

"You bought this here box?"

"Paid fifty cents for it," he asserted, failing to realize he'd now lumped himself with those *foolish* people. "It's a crime, isn't it?"

"Sounds like it could be. Tell you what, Jim. I'm on my way to another appointment. You go get Squire Fegley to swear out a warrant on this fellow and I'll see what I can do about it."

****

I slipped into a pew at the darkened rear of the church. The minister and the choir were busy up front and I didn't think any of them noticed me come in. That suited me just fine. I was content to watch and listen unobserved. Lydia was finishing up a solo of *Heavenly Sunlight*, one of her favorite hymns.

Leaning back and shutting my eyes, I focused on her lovely voice as it swelled into the nooks and crannies of the old church building:

Ever I'm walking close to His side.

The choir joined in on the refrain:

In the bright sunlight, ever rejoicing,
Pressing my way to mansions above;
Singing His praises gladly I'm walking,
Walking in sunlight, sunlight of love.

I'll admit, I'm not the most God-fearing man. But sitting there in the quiet dark and listening to those words, I was moved. Maybe it was just the solace the words offered in the wake of the horrendous deeds of the past two days. I don't know. Yet I experienced a spell of calm and was content to believe there is a Greater Power watching over us.

I was seated there, eyes still closed, musing on these thoughts, when a rustle of skirts and a touch on my arm brought me back to the present.

"Syl," Lydia said, "how long have you been here?"

"Only a little while," I told her. "Your song was real nice."

She smiled. "Thank you," she said. Other choir members filed by, heading for the door. Lydia nodded to some and murmured "Good night" to others. I rose and took her arm and we followed toward the exit.

"What are you doing here?" she asked as we went out.

"Why I hadn't seen you all day and I thought I'd walk you home. That's all right, isn't it?"

She patted my hand and nestled closer. "Of course. That's very kind of you."

"My pleasure."

It was a blissful night. The moon had come up and the air was practically balmy in comparison with the night before. Dry, fallen leaves crackled underfoot. A scent of overripe grapes from someone's arbor hung in the air. The gas lamps along the way cast a warm glow across the street. They have some of those new electric arc lamps over at Shannon. I saw them on a recent visit. Their light seems harsh in contrast to the mellow luster of gas.

We walked along in silence for a moment. Then she asked, "Did you and Cyrus have a nice day?"

I didn't intend on spoiling things by admitting my dislike for her cousin. So I lied. "Great. We had lunch together and then he went to an autopsy with me."

She halted in mid-step. "An autopsy?"

I explained about Deibert.

"Oh, that poor man. And his wife. She seems such a frail little thing. How will she bear the loss?"

Her compassion was touching, but it came as no surprise to me. I'd seen it in action before and her empathy with the suffering of others is just one of the catalog of things I love about this girl.

"Mrs. Deibert has the support of your new pastor. Did you know he was tutoring her? Seems she missed out on schooling and her husband hired Huber for a teacher."

"Well I'm sure he can use the extra money. What the congregation pays him is a sin. It's almost as bad as the stingy manner in which the borough compensates you. I'm glad she has someone to lean on. That sister-in-law probably won't be much help. Oh, dear. That must sound un-Christian of me. I expect those women will need one another now."

Her remark about my salary stung and for a moment I considered whether it might be a factor in her rejection of my suit.

"How did Cyrus bear up at the autopsy?"

"Oh he did all right."

Lydia chuckled. "He's quite resourceful. Tougher than you might think."

I grunted. "What do you think about him?"

"Who? Cyrus?"

"No. I meant Reverend Huber. What do you know about him?"

"He seems a bit aloof but I suppose that's because he's new here. Reverend Tyler was with us a long time and it can take a while to adjust to another pastor. I'm sure he'll be fine when we get to know him. He isn't much as a choir director. Not really musical at all."

"Do you know where he was before he came here?"

"Dauphin County I believe. I'm not really sure."

That struck a chord with me. I wondered if he and the Deiberts had known one another before coming to Arahpot. It was another thing for me to check on. All of those matters would have to wait for the morrow. I stifled a yawn. Bed beckoned.

Too soon, we came to Lydia's door and I bade her goodnight. She bent and kissed me on the cheek. "Maybe I'll be able to make you a proper supper tomorrow," she whispered.

"That'd be nice."

Then she spoiled it.

"I'll invite Cy, too. You should get to know him better. He needs a job. Maybe you can convince him to be your new deputy."

OCTOBER 8, 1897

CHAPTER 11

The jury reached its verdict fast and, as before, it came as no surprise:

"Death by unnatural causes, specifically arsenic poisoning, whether the result of accident, intent or at the hands of person or persons unknown to be determined by further investigation."

So it was all up to me. I hate having little to do, but my plate was getting a bit too full for my liking with two suspicious deaths in only a matter of days. And I couldn't help thinking the two were somehow connected.

Though I believed Barbara Frey was telling the truth I still couldn't figure what reason Verbena Deibert could have had for wanting to meet with Conrad Runkle. And I couldn't see that pretty little thing stabbing the man any more than I believed it possible her late husband had done it.

It was a conundrum I wasn't ready to deal with just yet.

Since Doc had already spoken to the pharmacist, I decided to pay a visit to Ollie Kintzler. It seemed like as good an opportunity as any to see what light he might shine on the situation.

The old man dwelt in a tumble-down house out in the country a little ways past the Deibert farm.

A warming trend had moved in over night. Clouds hung high in a blue sky. Though the fields along the way were sere there was color in the trees on the mountainside and thickets of crimson sumac seed heads and the blue of Joe Pye weed added a pretty contrast.

Though my purpose was not, it was a nice day for a ride in the country. It might have been especially pleasant had I been taking my best girl for a ride and not about to ask a man did he have a hand in poisoning another.

Kintzler's place was the last on a narrow road which forked off to the left, then circled around to rejoin the main route back to town. The lane served no other purposes save a means of egress to his residence. Which, I supposed, was its intent.

So-called modern folk in town scoff at pow-wowing as superstition but I know a lot of them sneak out here every now and again to consult Ollie Kintzler when other more conventional remedies fail to heal their ails. Doc doesn't believe in it, but my daddy did. He often told me, "Son, don't dismiss a thing out of hand until you've seen it don't work." I thought that good advice. I've never had occasion to ask for a cure, but I've seen some funny things and I know lots of folks who swear hexing worked when nothing else did.

Kintzler was in an old rocker on what passed for a porch. He stood as I pulled up and gave me a stiff salute. "Something I can do for you, Sheriff?" he asked in a crackly voice.

I dismounted, tied up and walked over to where he stood. "Nice day."

"Won't last."

"They never do."

Kintzler was a little mite of a fellow, barely five feet tall and so thin a good wind might have blown him away. He had snow white hair and chin whiskers (the latter of which showed the stain of tobacco juice). He squinted up at me with blue eyes made large by gold-framed spectacles. "Asked if I could do something for you. Or are you just out for a joy-ride today?"

I leaned with one hand on a porch post and gazed back at him. "I'm here to ask if you know Valentine Deibert?" I won't say I fear the man, but I've heard stories. I was putting on a brave front, but I'll admit my legs felt shaky and that may have been the reason I sought the post for support.

"The one bought the Schneider farm? Sure. I know him. What about it?"

"Did you treat him?"

"I don't talk about my patients," he said, surly-like.

"This one's dead."

That caught him by surprise, though he tried not to show it. I saw it in the widening of his eyes and a little jerk of his head. "I cure folks, not kill'em."

"I didn't say how he died. You ever give him arsenic?"

Kintzler shook his head slowly, side to side. "I don't use tinctures. I heal people with words. Ask anybody."

"I'm not accusing you of anything, sir. Just following up on some leads. The man stopped going to Dr. Mariner. Someone said they thought he might have come to you."

The old man relaxed then and shook his head. "He did. But he wouldn't listen to me any more than he did Mariner. Man was a fool who thought he had diseases when he didn't. If he'd had sick I could have healed him."

"How long ago did he stop coming to you?"

"Only came once. Must have been three-four weeks ago."

"And he didn't look sick to you then?"

"He was a man ate too much of the wrong things. That's a bad habit, not an ailment."

"Do you know if he saw anyone else?"

He leaned over and spat off the porch. "How would I? I mind my own business. People don't take my advice I don't care where they choose to go." That was the end of our conversation. Kintzler turned and went back in his house.

Man hadn't offered me a coffee or nothing. Don't know if I'd have accepted anyway. I got back on my rig and headed for town.

****

"I already told you everything I know," Barbara Frey said, backing away.

I found the girl sweeping the same steps where I'd first talked to Matilda that other day. Barbara held out the broom before her like it was a staff to ward me off.

"Easy, girl," I told her. "I'm not here to harass you. I just want to clarify a few things. I promise, you're not in any trouble."

Barbara lowered the broom and leaned on it. "She denied it, didn't she?"

I nodded.

"So you believe her and not me. Just because she has money..."

She pouted and I felt sorry for the girl.

"Didn't say that, did I? Come here, sit a minute." I went by her and sat on the steps. Barbara hesitated a moment, then she joined me, sitting a little closer than I wanted. But at least I knew now she wasn't going to run off as I'd feared she might.

"There are a few points we haven't discussed."

"Like what?" she asked, her eyes darting at me.

"Like why did Mrs. Deibert come to you in the first place?"

"How the hell should I know? She just did. Why don't you ask that preacher?"

"Reverend Huber?"

She nodded, gnawing on her lower lip. "If that's his name. I see them around together all the time. He's the one brought her."

"He was with her?"

"Not that night. But earlier in the day when they came here. She didn't know me. He knew my name and where I worked. I don't know how. He just did. She was all nervous like, so he did most of the talking."

"This was here?" I said, indicating the boarding house.

"Uh-huh."

"Did anyone else see them? Matilda or Lizzie?"

Barbara shook her head. "No. Lizzie was out and Tillie was in back, working on her books."

"So he brought her here and made the introductions. But he wasn't there that night?"

Barbara gave me a sour look. "Are you deaf or something, Sylvester? That's what I've been saying."

"Okay. Okay. I'm not doubting your word. I just want to be clear on things."

"Well then pay attention to what I'm saying. How many times do you expect me to say things?" She pushed a lock of hair back behind one ear.

Gravel crunched underfoot in the alley-way between the boarding house and the neighboring structure. We both turned to look and in a moment Billy Thew, a local drunk, stumbled out, passed us without a glance and went on down the street.

Barbara gnawed a thumb nail, gave me a pleading look and asked, "You done asking questions now?"

"One more thing. I want you to tell me as clearly as you remember what they said to you that day."

She raised her eyebrows and blew air. "As if I didn't already a million times. I was told to find out where Runkle would be that night and let her know. Then I was to tell him she wanted to talk to him. She paid me two dollars in advance for doing it. That's the whole of it."

"Not quite. How did you know where to find her?"

"She told me where she'd be waiting in her carriage."

"She was the one driving the carriage?"

"I guess so. It didn't get there on its own."

"Did he recognize her name when you gave him the message?"

"He must have. He came right away."

"And you didn't see anyone else lurking around when he came out?"

"I didn't go with him. I pointed out where he was to find her and then I went home."

****

I didn't have the warrant for the flimflam doctor yet but I thought I'd check him out. A plump, bald man, badly in need of a shave and with a nose as red as a strawberry, he stood in his wagon-bed and ran off a well-rehearsed spiel to a goodly crowd of onlookers.

"Gather round, my friends," he crowed. "This is my clever compound," and he held a container like Baker's aloft. "Guaranteed to cure all diseases—with the possible exception of hog cholera, for which there is yet no remedy."

Cyrus Gutshall was standing to one side of the crowd, a grin on his mug. I sidled up to him. "Buy yours yet?"

He swiveled a look at me. "Not likely. The man's a crook, but the suckers have been biting hard all week. It's been part of my entertainment here in your fair community. But the entertainment value is wearing thin. He gives an amateurish ventriloquist performance, passes out some free samples of a liquid potion, then reels them in for this stuff. You gonna arrest him?"

I shrugged. "Waiting on a warrant. I've only had one complaint. Thought I'd check him out."

Gutshall gave me a hard look. "Don't wait too long. I think he's running short on customers. He'll soon be in the wind."

****

The Good Book says man does not live by bread alone. Maybe so, but it does make for a pleasant end to a day. I was relishing some fine homemade bread and all that went with it for an excellent meal that evening at Lydia's. I wasn't even lamenting the presence of her abominable cousin. Truth is—despite having two vexing investigations before me—I was in a good mood.

"You seem cheerful tonight, Sylvester," Lydia said, passing me a bowl of mashed potatoes. "Does that mean you're closer to solving those murders?"

"No. But I got me some good leads today. Could I have the gravy, please?"

Mrs. Longlow sent it around via her husband who passed it to Gutshall. He reached it across to me. "I never would have thought there'd be so much excitement in a little place like this," he said.

"Usually isn't," I told him, not wanting to encourage the possibility of his asking for the deputy job. "Most times life in Arahpot is just plain boring."

"Now, Syl," Lydia said, a scowl on her pretty face, "you know that isn't true. This is a nice place to live."

"I didn't say it wasn't. I just said it can be boring at times. Could I have the cauliflower?" Lydia's pot roast is just about the most succulent I ever tasted and I kept quiet for a few minutes to give my full attention to the food.

"That boy Simon told me you went to see a pow-wow doctor today," Gutshall said.

I snapped a look at him and nodded.

"Ollie Kintzler?" Mr. Longlow said. "Is he still alive?"

"And full of vinegar," I told him.

"You think he poisoned that man?" asked Gutshall, laying down his fork.

"Kintzler heals folk," Lydia's father told him. "He doesn't kill them. And he does it with words, not potions."

"That's exactly what he told me."

"Then why'd you go to see him?"

"Because I knew Deibert had been to see him and an investigator has to look into everything."

"Could I have that gravy back?"

I gave it to him.

"All this talk of murder is not proper supper-table conversation," Mrs. Longlow said. "Why don't we talk of something more pleasant?"

And so we did for the rest of the meal.

Afterwards we retired to the parlor for coffee. Lydia, Gutshall and me played a board game while Mrs. Longlow knitted and her husband dozed in his chair. It was near ten o'clock when I took my leave and started home.

I had just opened my gate and started up the walk when I heard my name called. I turned and saw Clara Mariner crossing from her yard.

"Hello, Clara. You're keeping late hours."

"I was watching for you," she said, coming up to my gate.

"You were? What can I do for you?"

"That poor Mrs. Runkle," Clara said, glancing back at her own house. "You know she's near destitute?"

"Yeah?"

"Her husband needs burying and she can't afford to ship him back to Lancaster. Even if she could, they don't have a burial plot and she doesn't have the money to bury him. So we've decided to take up a collection, buy a plot at the cemetery and bury him here."

"You and Hiram?"

"No. The Ladies Aide Society from the church. Don't you think it's a wonderful idea?"

"Sure. The woman agreeable to this plan?"

"Yes, and grateful."

"So, what do you need from me?"

"A donation, of course. I know you don't have a lot of money. But anything you can give would be appreciated."

I dug in my pocket and came up with a fifty cent piece. I handed it to her. "It haint much but..."

Clara took the offering. "It all adds up. We had a good response at the church today and Lydia is going to put a collection container at the store."

Then it occurred to me. The Mariners attended the Methodist church, too. "What can you tell me about your new pastor?"

"Reverend Huber. Why?"

"Just curious. Lydia says he came from Dauphin County, same as the Deiberts. I was wondering if they might have been acquainted before coming here."

"Oh, I think Lydia's mistaken about that. I'm pretty sure Reverend Huber said he was in York before. You might ask him yourself, though. He's agreed to bury the man tomorrow. You'll be attending the service, won't you?"

"Yes. I will." I needed to talk to that preacher anyway.

OCTOBER 9, 1897

CHAPTER 12

As usual, the service dragged on too long with the usual maudlin preaching, the sobbing and the commenting on what a good person the deceased had been—despite the fact few had a good word for the poor devil when he was alive. I had expected less of the latter since Runkle had only been in town a short time. But those attending still found plenty to say about the man. I guess you might say it was a good send-off for the departed. Still I think he might have appreciated all the attention more when he was still around to hear it.

The service drew a larger crowd than I expected, too. Some were members of the congregation testifying to their charity in contributing to the man's burying, others were local merchants flaunting their community service in the same manner. Of course the Mariners, the Longlows and Gutshall were on hand along with the widow and me. Verbena Deibert came, probably in respect of her loyalty to the pastor. And Matilda Rebuck and Barbara Frey also made an appearance, though they kept to the background and left before the meal served by the Ladies Aide Society afterward in the church hall.

Reverend Huber proved more verbose than I'd expected. Even the widow seemed anxious for him to get it over with. More than once I saw her look up, sigh and commence sobbing again as the minister continued his citations of the man's character and virtue. Lydia said afterward she thought it a wonderful tribute. Maybe it was and my impatience was just the result of my desire to confront Huber with some questions.

It took a while before I got him alone. He disappeared into the church as soon as the sexton and his helper commenced shoveling dirt on the coffin they'd lowered into its hole. Not wanting to appear disrespectful, I waited with the mourners until that was attended to. Then we all filed into the hall for the luncheon. I was looking around for Huber when Lydia called me over. She and her mother, Clara and the Mariner girls were all helping serve the meal.

"Aren't you going to eat?" Lydia asked.

"Sure. But I was looking for Pastor Huber. I need to talk to him."

"He took Mrs. Deibert home. I guess she wasn't up to staying. It was nice of her to come though, wasn't it? You better get in line before all the good food is gone. We weren't expecting this many people."

My stomach rumbled and I thought maybe she was right. "Okay. But I have to talk to Huber."

"He'll be back. I'm sure of it. You can talk to him later. Now go get some food. You're looking peaked."

Given the number of people milling about I supposed she was right. I headed for the line which extended out into the corridor and was glad when Hiram Mariner spied me and waved me into place next to him. "Nice service," he said.

"If you're into that kind of thing. Me, when my time comes, I hope it'll get done with a whole lot less fuss."

"Don't give me that. You crave attention as much as the next man."

"Sure, when I'm alive to appreciate it. Where's Simon?" I had just missed seeing the boy.

"Things like this upset the lad. He lost his Pa early but he's still not over missing his mother."

I nodded. Doc and his family had taken the boy in after his mother's passing last spring. We came up on the first of the food now. There was a lot, but with the crowd behind us it might not be enough for all. I thought about the parable of the Lord and the fishes. I didn't think Huber was up to matching that miracle and there'd be some people leaving here today with empty bellies.

The selection was good: oyster sandwiches, cold tongue, chicken salad, funeral beans and macaroni salad, chow-chow, pickles and beets, a good selection of biscuits and cakes, all to be washed down with your choice of coffee, tea or chocolate. I walked along, selecting as much as I could from platters and servers I recognized as belonging to Lydia and Clara. I noticed the preacher was back as I was finishing a second slice of apple pie topped with cheese. "Reverend Huber," I called, setting aside my plate and heading toward him.

"Good afternoon, Sheriff. Getting enough to eat?"

"I've had my fill. Have you eaten?"

"I had lunch with the Deiberts. I was just going to get a cup of coffee."

"I'll join you. Then maybe you and me could have a little talk."

He threw me a surly glance. "Now? What about?"

"I thought you could help me clear up a couple things."

We breached the line and got our coffee. He headed out into the hall and I followed. "I'll be glad to help if I can. Shall we go outside? It's a bit stuffy in here."

We left the building and found seats on the wall surrounding the cemetery. It was another fine autumn day and we might have appeared two friends enjoying a coffee in the open. The sun was warm on our flesh, there was the odor of fresh-turned earth in the air (never mind its source), juncos and chickadees chirped in the churchyard and a chipmunk was busy stocking its granaries farther along the wall. It was a nice afternoon.

But, of course, we weren't friends, Huber and I. "How long have you been here now?" I asked.

He contemplated a moment. "I suppose it must be three-four months."

"You and the Deiberts seem particularly close."

He regarded me suspiciously over the rim of his cup. "They've been faithful members of my flock and, as I told you before, Valentine provided me with additional employment."

"They were here a little before you."

"Yes. I believe that's true."

"Did you know them previously?"

The question drew his full attention. "Is there a reason you ask that?"

I shook my head. "No more than idle curiosity. Did you?"

He lowered his eyes, turning round his cup in his hands. "No." The answer came so softly it was nearly a whisper.

"I've been told you and the Deiberts came here from Dauphin County."

He raised his head and looked at me again. "What of it? Many people come from the same place."

"Did you know one another there?"

"I said we hadn't met before."

"You did live in Dauphin County then?"

"Yes."

"Odd. Someone else said you came here from York County."

His eyes fixed on me but there was no change in his placid expression. "I have served there in the past. Perhaps your informant was confused as to where I was last."

That was possible, but Clara Mariner was seldom wrong in her assertions. I thought her more likely to be certain of a matter like this than Lydia whose concern was usually more with the present than the past. I changed tack now.

"Do you think it possible Mrs. Deibert might have poisoned her husband?"

This question did produce a change in his demeanor. The man paled and he spun around so abruptly he dropped his empty cup which shattered on the ground. "How can you make such an absurd statement? Verbena loved the man."

He stood up. I noticed his hands were shaking.

I smiled. "It was merely a question, not an accusation."

He cleared his throat and swallowed. "More of your idle curiosity?"

"You might say that."

"Well, I've had enough of it for one day. I've got to get back inside." And he strode off.

I might have pursued him. I didn't. I was satisfied just to have rankled the smug bastard.

****

Lydia had reopened the store after the service and luncheon. En route back to my office I stopped by to see if I had any mail. Among the usual county notices, wanted posters and similar truck there was a letter with a familiar heading. I tore it open and stood in the light by the front window to read it.

Dear Sheriff Tilghman,

In response to your recent telegraphic inquiry, yes, we did dispatch a letter to Mister Conrad Runkle last month in relation to an investigation he had commissioned with our firm.

The epistle was to inform him of the whereabouts of a certain Phoebus Potteiger, who he was seeking. Our agents discovered the aforesaid Mister Potteiger had been seen in Harrisburg, Dauphin County, this state, but had recently left there, apparently intent on joining his wife who our agent learned had previously departed for your community.

We are always ready to cooperate with law enforcement officials. Should you require additional information on this issue, please do not hesitate to call upon us.

At your service, yours sincerely,
Albert Casey,
President,
Casey Detective Agency
We Catch Those We Go After

Postscript-Should you be in contact with heirs of Mister Runkle, please remind them he still owes us a sum for said investigation.

Wife? I recollected the frightened look on Deibert's face that day in this store. Could Casey have been referring to him and Verbena? But, no. That didn't make sense. The Deiberts had arrived in Arahpot together. Then who was this Phoebus Potteiger?

"You look as though you swallowed something not to your liking, Syl." Lydia interrupted now. "Was it something you ate at the luncheon?" She'd come up to my side without my noticing.

"What? Uh-no. Just a thought stirred up by this letter."

She looked over my shoulder. I folded the letter and held it down by my side, not so much because I was annoyed by her curiosity as I was desirous of keeping this new information to myself for the time being.

"Aren't you going to let me see it?" she asked, vexed.

"Not right now. I've got to go." I started for the door.

"Syl."

I swiveled round, facing her. "Humph?"

My girl stood with her hands on her hips, her eyes blazing at me. "This is the first time I can remember you didn't share something with me."

"Sorry. It wasn't intentional. I'm just perplexed about something. When I get some answers I'll tell you all about it."

"Maybe I can provide some of those answers. What is it has you all bothered?"

I hesitated a moment, then blurted, "You ever hear of a man called Phoebus Potteiger?"

She wrinkled her pretty forehead. "No. I don't think so."

"Then you don't have the answer I need. I'll see you later." And I continued out the door.

****

Catherine Deibert opened the door to my first knock.

"Good afternoon, Miss Deibert. Is your sister-in-law home?"

She shook her head. "They've gone to town."

"They?"

"Her and the minister."

I'd assumed that might have been who she meant. "May I come in? I have a few questions."

"As you wish." She turned and strode down the hall. I followed. This time she led me back to the kitchen and indicated I should take a seat at the table. The fragrant perfume of fresh-baked bread hung in the air. Catherine sat opposite and I noticed for the first time her eyes were red and her cheeks swollen. The woman had been crying.

"Would you like some coffee, Sheriff?"

I recalled her coffee hadn't been very good. "No, thank you. I just wanted to pay my respects and I had a few questions..."

"They went to settle up on the arrangements. I wasn't ...I wasn't up to it." Her voice quivered. "I expect they'll be going to the lawyer, too. About his will. I suspect he changed it. If he did," she gave a wheezing sigh, "if he did, I don't know what'll become of me."

"If this isn't a good time, I could come back."

Catherine snuffled, drew a handkerchief from her sleeve and dabbed at her eyes. She gazed across at me. "This is as good a time as any. What did you want to ask?"

Sometimes the job makes us less sensitive than we should be. I felt sorry for the woman. I reached out and touched her arm. "I'm sure your brother will have provided for you. You were very close, weren't you?"

"We were the last of our family."

"I'm sure this is difficult for you. Were you told the cause of your brother's death?"

"Why I suppose it was all his ailments, wasn't it?" she asked, wiping her eyes.

"The cause of death was arsenic poisoning."

My comment startled her. She stared at me with widened eyes and mouth agape. Her body shook and I feared she might faint. "I never thought..."

"Does that surprise you?"

"I think I need coffee," she said, getting up and going to the stove. "Won't you have some, too?"

I didn't want it, but I told her I'd take a half cup.

She brought the coffee and sat again.

"The pharmacist in town, Mr. Hockenbroch, he told Doctor Mariner your brother purchased a lot of medications. Some of those contain arsenic."

Catherine toyed with her cup and shook her head. "He didn't do this to himself."

"What are you telling me, Miss Deibert?"

"I saw *her* soaking flypapers in a basin. You know, to remove the arsenic."

I recalled what Lydia had told me about Verbena buying flypapers out of season. "Your sister-in-law?"

"Yes."

"Are you accusing her of poisoning your brother?"

She took a sip of coffee, then raised her eyes to meet mine. "I only tell you what I saw. I have no proof. That's for you to find."

"You're not fond of her, are you?"

Her eyes flashed and a frown twisted her features. "I'm not saying this simply because I dislike her. People see Verbena as docile and innocent. They don't realize how manipulative she can be."

"How so?"

"How?" Her voice raised in pitch and she sat her cup down on its saucer with such force I thought it might break. "She changed our lives. She took us away from what was familiar and brought us to this place where we are strangers and isolated from our former friends. If she'd had her way entirely I would have been left behind in Dauphin County. But Valentine wouldn't hear of that."

"Then it wasn't his idea to move here?"

"No. We had a life there. He had his business. We were content with our single state and supportive of one another before she came along. Then she intruded on our peace, convinced him to sell his business and retire."

"What was his business?"

"A mill and a granary started by our father. It was a prosperous business. It kept him occupied and happy. It was only after he gave it up his health problems began. If you look, I'm sure you'll find she was the cause of his death."

"It will be necessary to search the premises and see if arsenic similar to that which caused his death is present. I'll need to come back with authority to do that and with witnesses to affirm whatever might be found. Are you agreeable to that?"

"I am," she said firmly.

I rose. "I'll go and make the necessary arrangements. I probably won't be able to come back until tomorrow morning. Meanwhile, I'd suggest you say nothing to your sister-in-law about our conversation today. If she is guilty of this crime I don't want her to have the opportunity to destroy any evidence."

Catherine escorted me back to the front of the house. As I made to leave, another thought occurred to me. "Did you happen to know a man named Phoebus Potteiger back in Dauphin County?"

"No," she said, shaking her head. "Should I?"

OCTOBER 11, 1897

CHAPTER 13

Verbena's pretty face twisted into an ugly mask. "You have no right," she rasped, following us into her bedroom.

"Sorry, ma'am, but we do," Cyrus Gutshall told her before I had a chance to open my mouth. I shot him a look but he didn't even notice. We'd had to wait until Monday since October 10 was the Sabbath and Charlie Fegley couldn't get authorization from the county for the search earlier. I'd been given power to deputize Doc to assist me and needed another as witness. Gutshall had followed us to Charlie's office and the squire pointed out the man would do just fine if he was willing. Of course he was, to my chagrin.

Verbena's bedroom was our last stop on the search of the household. For once the minister wasn't present when we arrived at the farm. But Verbena proved vocal enough on her own in objecting to the search. "How dare you accuse me of harming my husband," she snarled. "I loved him. This is outrageous." She spun on Catherine. "Aren't you as upset about this as I? You know I worshiped your brother. I'd never have done anything to harm him. Tell them."

But Catherine kept her mouth shut and did her best to stay out of our way. Verbena, on the other hand, trailed after us from room to room and even went along when we went out to check the privy and the other outbuildings. At least that kept her from destroying anything while we were occupied elsewhere.

She became most agitated when we came at last to her bedchamber, standing in the doorway, twining her hands and nibbling her bottom lip. I was a little uncomfortable about that as well. I hadn't been in a woman's bedroom save for my mother's since I was a child. It made me nervous just looking around and seeing all the fluff and frippery. In comparison, Catherine's room had been neat and tidy—nothing out of place or inclined to bother a man. Verbena's room was a mess. The bed was unmade and the slop jar stood right out in the open where she'd used it earlier that morning. Besides the fancy toilet sets you'd expect to see in a woman's room, every surface was littered with stuff. She had a bigger collection of perfume containers and atomizers on her dresser than would have been found in Hockenbroch's pharmacy. They were joined by containers of powder and facial ointments, various homeopathic remedies, switches and braided hair rolls and jewelry containers spilling out their contents. If that wasn't enough, bits and pieces of clothing were strewn all over the room, including stockings, a nightgown and various unmentionables. It was enough to make the average man blush. I didn't see how Doc expected to find anything incriminating here.

"Found something," Gutshall said, kneeling and pointing behind a bureau.

"Don't touch it," Hiram told him. "Let me get it." With a gloved hand, he plucked a handkerchief from behind the bureau.

"She could have lost that a month ago and just forgot about it," I said.

"He's right," Verbena said. "That might be exactly right."

"Well," Doc said, "we'll just add it to our collection and see if it tells us anything different." He dropped the handkerchief into one of his collection bags which already held a variety of other things gathered from the kitchen, Catherine's room and other parts of the property. Mariner moved about the room, lifting lids and examining contents, sniffing vials and bottles.

Verbena came farther into the room and gave Gutshall a piercing look as he lifted the lid on her jewelry box. "If anything's missing I'll know where to send my lawyer."

"You'll have an inventory of every article we remove," he told her.

The audacity of the man. If it hadn't been for the others present I'd have been tempted to give him a smack. I was the one taking the inventory and with the authority to tell her what was what.

Finally the search was completed and we returned to the ground floor of the house. Verbena went back up the stairs, presumably headed for her room. Catherine walked with us out to my buggy. "Thank you for your cooperation, Miss Deibert," Doc told her and climbed up on the rig. Gutshall jumped in the back.

As I started around to my side, Catherine tugged at my sleeve. "I was right," she whispered, hoarsely. "She persuaded Valentine to change his will. He left everything to her and, worse, named Pastor Huber as executor. I'll be left out in the cold." There were tears glistening in her eyes.

What could I say? I did my best to console the woman, advising her to see a lawyer herself to see if the document might be challenged. But I'm no attorney and I didn't know if that was valid advice or not. I patted her arm and drove off, leaving the poor woman standing there in the road.

****

"How long will it be before you know anything?" I asked Hiram as we drove back to town.

"Might be a day or two. I've got several bags full of things here and I'll have to run tests on all of them to see if any trace shows up."

"She's a sprightly thing, haint she?" Gutshall said, looking back over his shoulder toward the farmhouse. "You think she done it?"

I wasn't inclined to answer and Doc kept his trap shut, too.

"Me, I'd be more suspicious of that sister," Gutshall added. "She has the look of a woman who could put poison in a man's tea."

Again I didn't reply. Despite my earlier opinion of Catherine I was now inclined to see her more as the victim than perpetrator. Still, a good investigator has to keep an open mind. Despite her claims of filial devotion, if Catherine had been aware of her brother's intent to change his will there was the possibility she might have been moved to vengeance. Neither woman could be ruled innocent yet.

****

"I'm an innocent man," Dr. A. E. Paul protested as I hauled him up before Squire Fegley. "This is outrageous."

I'd had a few more complaints by the time I got the warrant to arrest the flimflam man. I had other things on my mind but I knew if I didn't pick him up he'd be on his way to fleece people in other communities.

"You've been charged with false pretenses and swindling," Charley Fegley told the man. "I don't take kindly to people who charge citizens of my town fifty cents for a box of sawdust they could get for nothing at the local planing mill."

"It's not sawdust," Dr. Paul said, indignantly. "It's a preparation of great healing powers."

Charley held up a box of the stuff and peered into it. "Looks like sawdust to me. I'll give you a choice, sir. You can pay a fine and get out of town or go to trial and take a chance on spending some time in our lock-up."

Paul glowered and thought a moment. He glanced at me, then back at the squire. "If I pay the fine I can go?"

"That's what I said."

The man reached in his pocket and drew out a sheaf of bills. "How much? I'll pay now and shake the mud of Arahpot from my shoes immediately."

Charley fined him ten dollars plus cost and I escorted the man to the station. He caught the next train out. "It's too hot for me here," he said, climbing aboard.

****

Arahpot is a small town and strangers seldom go unnoticed. It kept nagging at me someone among our populace had to be aware of the appearance of the man called Phoebus Potteiger in town. If he'd been proceeded here by his wife, that meant two strangers to be accounted for. I didn't have an exact date for when Conrad Runkle was informed about it by the Casey Detective Agency. That meant I'd have to determine just when he came to Arahpot and work back from then. That entailed another visit to Matilda Rebuck's establishment.

"You're getting to be as common a presence here as my boarders," she said, cocking an eye at me in response to my knock. "What do you want this time?"

"I was wondering if you could tell me when Mister Runkle first took up residence here."

"You expect me to remember something like that?" She stepped back and ushered me into the hall. "I have people in and out all the time. I can't keep track of every Tom, Dick and Harry who stops by."

"Don't you keep some kind of records?"

Tillie glowered at me. "Only thing I need to know is whether they paid their rent or not. I don't have to write that down."

Fewer records for the taxman to know about, I thought. She's a wily bird, our Matilda. But I wasn't about to be put off. "I thought you'd at least know about when he came," I told her. "I'm trying to solve the poor man's murder. You were at the funeral. You saw the widow. Wouldn't you like to help me console her by bringing the man's killer to justice?"

"You're the lawman, not me. Come on back to the kitchen," she said, beckoning for me to follow. "Maybe one of the girls will have an idea. But you go easy on Barbara, you hear? Girl is scared enough as is."

"I mean her no harm."

Matilda cast a look back over her shoulder. "It's not you she fears," the woman told me.

The girls were seated at the table in the kitchen, peeling potatoes. Barbara gave me a wary look and Lizzie snapped, "You again."

I turned round another chair and straddled it facing them. "Me again. Matilda thought maybe you girls could help me with something."

"Who do you think we are, your deputies or something?" Lizzie quipped. Barbara didn't say a word, her attention fastened on the potato in her hand and which was being peeled deeper than its skin.

"If you've noticed, I don't have a deputy at present. Which explains why you're seeing more of me than somebody else on my account. If you're considering asking for the job I should advise you it doesn't pay much."

Lizzie wrinkled her nose and stuck out her tongue at me. "Wouldn't work for the likes of you if it did pay a lot."

Barbara giggled at that and Matilda clucked her tongue, apparently warning the girl to be more civil.

A big pot bubbled on the stove behind them, giving off a less than enticing odor.

"What's that you're cooking?"

"Lamb stew," Lizzie said, "and don't think you're getting an invitation to join us for supper."

"Wasn't planning on staying," I told her. I like my beef and pork. But lamb is right up there with goat as two animals I don't care to feed on. "I stopped by because I was hoping one of you might remember just when Mister Runkle took up residence here."

Lizzie cast a glance at Barbara who was still intent on peeling that spud. Matilda pulled out the chair next to me and sat down. "I thought you might recall," she said, reaching across and touching Barbara's arm. The girl looked up, her eyes flickering from her employer to me. "I don't know if I want to get more involved," she said.

"You're not in trouble, Barbara. I told you that before."

"Maybe not with you," she said in a little girl's voice.

"Has someone threatened you?"

She lowered her eyes and shook her head. "Not exactly."

"What *exactly* does that mean?"

"She went to visit a friend last night and somebody followed her," Lizzie said. "She came home scared out of her wits. That's what she means."

I wasn't sure if she meant an actual friend or if that was a euphemism for something else I didn't want to know about. "Did you see who it was?"

Barbara laid down the knife and the potato. Her face had gone pale and the girl was trembling. She clasped her hands together to still their shaking. "All I heard was footsteps behind me and all I saw was shadows. But I know they was after me. I ran all the way home."

"Her heart was beating like a little bird's," Matilda attested. "Girl was scared out of her wits."

"And you think it had to do with Runkle's murder?"

"Why, what else could it be?" Barbara asked, her eyes searching mine. "I haint done nothing to nobody else. I don't know if that lady killed him or not. But, whoever it was, I must have riled them up. I'm afraid to even go out to the privy at night now for fear I'll be next to have my throat cut."

"All the more reason you should do all you can to help me catch this person so your life can be peaceful again."

"Easy for you to say," Lizzie snapped.

I gave her a sympathetic nod. "You're right. I don't mean to be glib. I'm not the one in danger—not that I'm certain Barbara is. But she could be. I..."

"What do you mean, she could be?" Lizzie blurted. "Of course she is." And she laid down her knife and hugged her friend close. "If somebody's following her..."

"Will you let me finish, girl? I meant to say I'll do everything in my power to keep her safe. I don't think her cooperating with me is anything should warrant anyone wanting to harm her. But there are crazy people in this world. If I'd had a deputy I have him watching over you girls. Since I don't, I'll try and keep an eye on you as much as I can. Meanwhile I think none of you should venture outside alone at night. And Tillie, you do lock up at night?"

"When all my boarders are in at night. But I can't until they are."

"What was it you wanted to know?" Barbara asked, looking a little more reassured. "When Mister Runkle started staying here?"

"Yes. Do you remember?"

"Let me think on it a minute. I might recall."

Lizzie gripped her shoulder. "Barbie. You shouldn't..."

Barbara took her friend's hand. "It's okay. If it'll help Sylvester catch this fellow, then I got to try." She closed her eyes and leaned her head back. I could see a vein pulsing at the side of her long white neck and her eyelids twitched as she searched her memory.

She sat like that for a few moments more, then she nodded and pursed her lips. She opened her eyes and faced me. "I think it must have been a Thursday. Let me think. Matilda, where's your calendar?"

Tillie went and got a calendar that hung on the back of the door. She brought it back and handed it to the girl, who paged back to the previous month. Barbara dipped her head twice, then glanced over at me. "I think it must have been Thursday, the sixteenth of September."

"How can you be so certain about the date?"

Barbara flushed scarlet, her eyes darting from Matilda to Lizzie and then back to me. "I wouldn't say this kind of thing in front of just any man, Sylvester, but you being the law..."

"Yes?"

"Well I know because my period ended that day and he asked on Saturday...you know." She blushed again, then went on. "I wouldn't agree to that when I was still bleeding. But two days later, I was all clean again."

It was my turn to blush, but at least I understood her certainty.

CHAPTER 14

Dusk was descending when I left them. Our Indian Summer day had been replaced by a crisp autumn evening and, with the chill in the air that threatened frost by morning, I drew my coat close around me and was glad for it. I was nearly to the street when the glow of the lamp there cast a shadow across my path. I spun round just in time to see a figure dart around the side of Matilda's building.

Hurrying after him, I came into the yard in time to see a man skulking toward the back door. I crossed the space between us and caught him by the shoulder, spinning him around.

Lydia's cousin gawked at me. "What the..."

"What are you doing here?"

He caught himself, puffed out his chest and gawked at me. "I might ask you the same thing?"

"I saw you sneaking back here and I came after you. That's what. Now answer my question."

Gutshall sputtered a moment, then thought better of it. "Ah, what the heck. You know. I was in the army. I don't have a girlfriend like you. I..."

I felt my ears heat up and was glad he couldn't see them in the dim light. "Lydia and I don't...I mean..."

"Hey, it's none of my business anyway. I was just going to go in here and...you're not gonna tell her, are you?"

I shook my head. "No. You're a grown man. What you do on your own isn't my business either. Which one are you going to see?"

I couldn't make out his expression, but I'm sure he would have scowled just as I had a moment previously. "Not that it's your concern, but the pretty one of course."

"Good."

"Whadya mean good?"

I explained to him about Barbara's scare. "It may be nothing. But I wouldn't want any harm to come to the girl because I didn't take her seriously. Since you're seeing her anyway I wonder if I could count on you to help me out and keep an eye on Barbara and the other women of the household."

"Are you asking me to be your deputy?"

"No. I'm simply asking for a little help. It's my job to protect all the citizens of Arahpot, but I can't be everywhere at once. Will you do it?"

"Sure. All you had to do was ask."

****

"So, who do you think this man is?" Lydia asked.

Gutshall had told me she was keeping a plate warm for me, so I'd headed directly to her house when I left him. Lydia fed me in the kitchen and I was basking in these few moments alone with her since her elderly parents had already retired for the night. I'd told her about my day, including the new information about Phoebus Potteiger.

"I have no idea. But I did stop at the telegraph office this afternoon and send another message to that detective agency. I had informed them about Runkle's death. This time I asked if they had a description or a photograph of the man he was seeking."

"That makes sense. It should be easier to find the man if you know what he looks like."

I pushed my empty plate forward. "Is there any dessert?"

Lydia glowered at me. "You've put on some pounds lately, Sylvester. You should give more care to your health."

Chastened, I hung my head.

Then my love relented. "I did save you a piece of peach cobbler, though." She rose and got it. "Have you seen Cyrus tonight?" she asked, resuming her seat.

I took time for a swallow of the cobbler which, as I'd known it would, tasted delicious. "I-uh-asked him to help me with something."

"Oh? You deputized him?" She gave me a big smile.

"No. Not exactly. Just a task needed done and I couldn't handle alone."

She wrinkled her brow. "What might that be?"

I explained and Lydia scowled. "You might have found something more suitable. Those women have a reputation you know. My cousin puts on a brash front, but I think him really quite innocent of the real world."

I feigned a coughing fit to conceal my desire to laugh. *If she only knew the truth about her relative.* Well, I wasn't about to tread that dangerous path and inform her. Once I'd recovered I said, "I'm not asking him to keep company with them. Just to keep an eye on the house."

Lydia relaxed a bit then. She mulled the situation. Brushing a hand over her hair, she turned to me and asked, "Do you think they're really in danger?"

"I don't know. Barbara may be. At least she fears so. It may be nothing but her imagination. Still I didn't want to take the chance and have something happen to her or one of the others. You can understand that, can't you?"

"I suppose so. Yes. I can see you couldn't take it lightly. And you *do* need help. You can't watch over everyone in town twenty-four hours a day." She reached over and squeezed my arm. "Though you *do* try."

I shrugged. "It's my responsibility."

She gave me a direct look which forced me to lower my eyes.

"Cyrus would make you a good deputy."

Moving crumbs across the tabletop with my forefinger, I replied, "He hasn't asked for the job."

"But you'd consider it if he did?"

Reluctantly, I nodded.

"Well, good!" Lydia said and clapped her hands together. "I'm glad that's settled then." She picked up my empty dishes and utensils and carried them to the sink. Then she came back and sat next to me. "What will you do next?"

"I suppose I'll ask around and see if anyone can recall strangers in town."

"But you don't know when."

"Right."

"And you don't have a description of the man."

I nodded. "Granted I'm hoping it will be easier once I have a reply from the detectives."

"Of course. Right now, without those aids, it seems an impossible task. There are strangers passing through all the time. Often they come in the store. But if you can't tell me if the person you're looking for was in last week, or last month, or six months ago—how can I be expected to help you?"

"It does seem impossible."

A chunk of wood burned through and crackled in the stove.

"You need to know a time period." Lydia leaned her chin on one hand, its fingers caressing her pretty lip.

"Well I know now when Runkle arrived. It was sometime prior to that."

"That doesn't narrow it down much."

"True." It seemed an impossible task until I had a description before me.

OCTOBER 12, 1897

CHAPTER 15

It was a dismal, overcast day for the burial of Valentine Deibert and attendance was noticeably less than that for Conrad Runkle. Since the man was so little known in town they'd dispensed with the usual house-viewing, just as they had for Runkle, and held everything on the same day at the church. As before, Huber conducted the service. Verbena and Catherine sat at the front of the church, though one couldn't fail to notice several seats separated them. Hank Schneider and his wife came, Doc and I were there, a few of the more prominent members of the congregation and, I was surprised to notice, Ollie Kintzler, sitting by himself in a rear pew.

Like I said, I'm not a regular church-goer. But I noted some puzzled expressions and figured I wasn't the only one didn't recognize the text of Huber's sermon, which concluded:

"*Treat your friend well before you die, and reach out and give to him as much as your strength permits. Will you not leave the fruits of your labors to someone else?*"

At the conclusion of the service and before going out to the churchyard, Catherine announced there would be a meal available at the house and all were invited. Hiram whispered to me that the welcome probably didn't extend to us and I was inclined to agree. He said I was welcome to join the Mariners for lunch. I told him I'd meet him at his place after I had words with a few people.

One of the first I took time to seek out was old Kintzler.

"Didn't expect to see you here, old man."

"Man was a patient, even if he didn't pay my advice no never mind," Kintzler said, wheeling on me. "Why shouldn't I pay my respects?"

"No reason I can define. Just didn't think you liked the man."

"Don't have to like a man to respect his passing." Without a backward glance he strode away then.

It had commenced to rain while we were in the church, fat, stinging, cold drops that sent most of those who'd attended the service running off before the burying. I hung on to see it out, shivering in the damp despite my heavy coat and turned up collar. Huber didn't waste too many words and got the job over with as quick as could be done with dignity. As we filed toward our conveyances, I felt a tug on my arm.

I turned and faced Catherine Deibert. She looked up at me pathetically, her eyes reddened and her pale face streaked with dried tears under her black bonnet. "Will you arrest her?" she asked.

"I'm sorry, ma'am. The evidence isn't in yet."

"She killed my brother. You know it as well as I." She pivoted on her heel and walked off with bowed head and slumped shoulders.

****

"What was that text he used?" I asked Mariner as I tore off a chunk of bread and used it to sop up the last broth of chicken corn soup from the bowl before me.

"You know," he said, staring at me across the table, "it sounded vaguely familiar, but I just couldn't place it. I couldn't wait till I got home and rooted through my library. And, finally, I found it."

"It wasn't from the Bible, dear?" Clara asked, refilling our coffee cups.

"No. Of all things it was from the *Apochrypha. Ecclesiasticus*, to be exact. *The Wisdom of Sirach*, as it's sometimes called. But he did some paraphrasing, changing things around."

"That's stuff not in the regular Bible, right?"

"Books of doubtful origin. They're not usually in the Protestant Bibles."

"Why in blazes would he use something like that?"

"I don't know. I assume he was referring to Mrs. Deibert as the friend and justifying her inheriting everything while the poor sister is left with nothing."

"Speaking of the sister, Catherine asked when I'm going to arrest Verbena. Any answers on the arsenic yet?"

Hiram shook his head. "You'll have to be patient, Syl. There were a lot of samples and it takes time to run all the tests. And I can't neglect my practice, you know. My patients deserve attention as much as a dead man."

I took a sip of my coffee before replying. "I know. It's just that it's frustrating."

He gave me a sympathetic glance. "Be that as it may, I've got to beg your patience a little longer."

****

Back in my office after lunch, I was both bored and frustrated. Rain continued to fall, drumming on the roof of the building like the heartbeat of an agitated man. I'd been soaked again getting here and the odor of damp wool permeated the damp air of the room. Shivering with the chill, I sneezed. All I needed was to have a cold coming on. With a sigh I rose and lit a fire in the potbellied stove. Though I didn't need it, I put the coffee pot on to boil, too.

Returning to my seat I picked up the handful of new mail and fanned through it. Nothing from the detective agency. I dropped the post atop a scattering I hadn't bothered with from the day before. I'd scanned it casually earlier and saw it was mostly more wanted posters and other government notices. Since there was nothing better to do at the moment, I decided I might as well sort it all out. Paperwork has a tendency to pile up if you neglect it.

With a cup of coffee at hand, I tended to the task and in short order had pared it down—keepers going to one side of my desk, junk going into the trash can under the desk. It was routine, this activity, and my mind wandered, drifting from the two cases before me, to Lydia, thoughts of dinner, and back again. I was nearing the bottom of the stack when I came across a pardon notice. I was about to push it to one side when a date and a name caught my attention. I picked the sheet up and gave it closer scrutiny.

And that brought a smile to my face.

Grabbing my sopping cap and wet coat, I made for the door.

****

"Where is he?"

"Who?" Ollie Kintzler asked.

"You know blame well *who*. Now are you going to let me in, or must I stand out here in the rain?"

The old man had opened the door just a crack at my knock. His bushy eyebrows shot up now and he opened his mouth as though about to speak. But, apparently changing his mind, he thrust the door open wider and ushered me in.

"You don't have no right bothering us," he said, shutting the door behind me. "He's pardoned and he's come home to get a fresh start on his life."

I'd been admitted directly to the front room of the cabin. A lamp with a poorly trimmed wick sat on a nearby table and gave off a flickering light and a foul odor of kerosene. In the dim light, I saw the room was sparsely furnished with the table, a couple of wooden chairs and a cupboard against the far wall.

"I just need to talk to him."

"What about?" came a voice out of the dark and a figure stepped out from beside the cupboard. He crossed to the table, pulled out a chair and dropped onto it. I went and sat opposite him. There were plates and the remnants of food on the table. I must have disturbed them at their meal.

Christopher Kintzler, the old man's son, stared at me sullenly. He was a man of medium height, balding and stoop-shouldered, with a narrow face, bushy eyebrows like his father's and a ragged mustache.

"You were in Eastern Penitentiary," I said, referring to the prison in Philadelphia.

"Pardoned."

"Accused of fraud."

"Proven innocent. That's why the governor granted my pardon."

"How long have you been back here?"

He scratched at his chin with an audible rasp. "What's it to you?"

I leaned forward and matched his stare. "Look, you can cooperate or not. It doesn't matter to me. But if you don't cooperate I might see fit to charge you with another crime."

That took the starch out of him. He pulled back, licking his lips. "What crime? I haint done nothing."

"A man was stabbed here the other night."

"What's that got to do with me?"

"He died."

"And you think I done it?"

"Tell him, boy," Kintzler said, taking the seat next to mine. "You got nothing to hide."

He looked at his father and shook his head. "Law wants to accuse a man of something he didn't do, they have a way of doing it. I learned that by experience."

"I'm not after no innocent man," I told him. "I just have some questions need answering. You answer them to my satisfaction and I'll leave you be."

He wagged his head again. "Yeah. That's what they told me down in Harrisburg, too. And look what that got me."

"So you admit, your crime was in Dauphin County?"

"Wasn't my crime," he growled. "I was proved innocent."

"But the incident occurred there?"

He nodded.

"When did you get back here?"

Kintzler looked at his father. He scratched at his chin again and ran a hand over his head. "What? Sometime in May."

"Closer to the end of it," the old man said.

"And your wife?"

He looked at me, frowning. "Wife? I haint got no wife. Not no more. She left me when I was first accused."

"She's not here then?"

He shrugged. "I got no idea where she might be. And I don't care neither."

"When did you first meet Conrad Runkle?"

"Who?"

"The man who was stabbed."

"Never. I didn't know the man."

"Did you know Valentine Deibert?"

Kintzler looked at his father again. "Pa went to his funeral this morning. He bought our neighbor's farm. I never met him neither. What's he got to do with this?"

"Maybe nothing. It was just a question."

"Well I answered it. You got any more?"

"Not now. If I think of any you'll hear from me." I thought of something as I started to get up. "Wait. You been back so long how come nobody knew it? I haven't seen you around town."

"Them what needs to know does. I'm a tinker. People need work done they come here. Haint much need for me to go to town. Pa's company is mostly what I crave for now. I mind my own business."

As I started toward the door, Ollie Kintzler scuttled up to me, leaned close and whispered, "Weddar far grankeet ufflese."

I didn't know what they meant, but the words sent a chill through me.

OCTOBER 13, 1897

CHAPTER 16

"Gesundheit," Mrs. Longlow said in response to my sneeze.

"Yes," Lydia added, "bless you. Are you coming down with a cold?"

"I think so," I told her, wiping my nose with my hanky. I'd stopped by for a cup of coffee and, hopefully, an invitation to breakfast on the pretense of expecting Cyrus Gutshall might be there. I got my invite and was informed Gutshall was coming by for breakfast, also. "Do you happen to remember any of your German?" I asked Lydia. That's what we call the vernacular our Pennsylvania Dutch use among themselves.

"Very little, but mother does. Why?"

I told them about my visit with the Kintzlers. "As I was leaving the old man said something that's got me worrying a little."

"What was it? I'm sure mother can translate for you."

"Of course I can," Mrs. Longlow said. "That's all we spoke at home when I was a girl. Can you remember what he said?"

"I wrote it down as close as I could remember soon as I had a chance." I pulled a little slip of paper from my watch pocket and read, "*Weddar far grampkids arful.* Does that make sense?"

Mrs. Longlow began to giggle, covering her mouth with one hand. Mr. Longlow went even better. He snuffled, snorted and nearly dropped his coffee cup. "What?" I asked. "Did I say it wrong?"

Lydia laid her hand on mine and gave me a consoling smile. "You'll have to forgive my parents. They're easily amused these days."

Mrs. Longlow stopped chuckling and imitated her daughter's smile. "I'm sorry, Syl. I didn't mean to laugh, but I couldn't help it. You got the gist near enough for me to understand."

"But, I'm sorry, lad," her husband put in. "You'll not win any prizes for language aptitude."

"What he said to you, I'm sure, was: *weddar far grankeet ufflese*," Mrs. Longlow said. "It means *weather to catch disease.*"

"That's it. That's it in a nutshell, Mrs. L. So the old man's put a hex on me."

"Oh, no. I don't think so. He's not that kind of man. He probably was just commenting on the weather," she said.

"No. He didn't like me pestering his son. I'm sure he meant to put a spell on me."

"Syl," Lydia said, condescendingly, "you're not a superstitious person. Why would you think such a ridiculous thing?"

"Well, I didn't have this cold before I went out there, did I?" I knew I had been sneezing before my visit to Kintzler but it's easy to overlook fact when you're inclined to believe in foolishness.

"You were running around all day in the rain. I'm sure you were soaked and got a chill. That's where your cold came from."

"That's right, Sylvester," her mother said. "You're not *verhext*. You just need some more food. And take some tea with lemon and honey before you go to bed tonight."

Lydia snorted beside me. I threw her an angry look and she busted out giggling. It was another minute before she got herself under control and apologized. "I'm sorry. I just couldn't help it. Sylvester Tilghman thinking he's been bewitched. It's just too funny." And she started laughing all over again.

I was saved more embarrassment when the kitchen door popped open and Cyrus Gutshall strode in. "Hello all," he bellowed, then bent over to peck his aunt on the cheek. "Got any more eggs?"

"There's oatmeal on the stove," Mrs. Longlow said. "Help yourself, Cyrus."

"Yuck. Hate that mush. Don't you have any eggs, Auntie?"

"I'll make you some," Lydia said, stifling another giggle and moving round to the stove.

"What's so funny, Cuz?" Gutshall asked, a puzzled look on his face.

"Never mind," I said, pushing out a chair for him. "Sit down and tell me you've been doing what I asked."

He hung his hat and coat on a rack in the corner before coming over and sitting. "Much as I can," he said, shortly.

"What does that mean? I told you, those women might be in danger. I'm depending on you..."

"Now wait, buster," he said, turning on me. "I said I'd help and I am. But I'm not being paid for this and I have my own needs to be met. I have been keeping watch, but there are times when I have to eat and sleep and tend to other bodily functions. Now if..."

"Boys, boys," Lydia said, stepping up and laying a hand on both our shoulders. "This won't do. Syl, if Cyrus said he'd help, I'm sure he will. But wouldn't it be better if you deputized him?"

"Maybe this is a test," I said, sourly. "To see if he's worthy of the job."

"I haint sure I'd want his old job," Gutshall countered.

That brought him Lydia's ire. "Cyrus, Sylvester wouldn't have asked for your help if he didn't need it. And if this is a test, maybe it's warranted. Now both of you think on these things whilst I get your eggs." She bustled back to the stove.

Both of us did calm down. Gutshall turned to me a minute or so later and said, "There is something funny I wanted to tell you about."

Lydia brought his eggs just then. He glanced over at me. "Let me get some food in me and then I'll explain as we walk down to your office."

"Neither of you plan on walking me to the store this morning?" Lydia asked.

"It's on the way," I told her. Conceding to her curiosity, I added, "and you can listen in as Cyrus tells me his news."

That bought me another smile.

****

"I thought I'd check on them one more time before going to bed," Cyrus explained as the three of us headed down the street. It was a much better day for a walk, a bright sun sopping up the moisture from the trees, fallen leaves and sodden lawns along the way. "It must have been nigh onto ten o'clock and there was no light showing from the house. I figured everyone must have retired and I was about to go back to my hotel and do the same."

"But something happened, Cousin?" Lydia asked, looking up at him expectantly.

"Yes," he said with a nod. "Just as I turned to leave, my eye caught a movement in the shadows at the side of the house. I stepped back in the dark against the building opposite and watched. In a moment, I saw a figure creep out and head down the street."

"Who was it?" I asked, as eagerly as Lydia.

"If you'll give me a minute, I'll get to it," he said, petulantly.

Despite my curiosity, I resolved to be patient. "Go on," I urged.

"I could tell it was a woman, but I couldn't make out who. I wondered if it might be Barbara Frey, though I figured if she was so frightened why would she come out at such an hour and where could she be going. So I decided to follow along for a while at a distance and see what was up. We hadn't gone more than another block or two than she passed under a lamp and I saw it was the other one. Lizzie—what's her name?"

"Lizzie Kline."

"That's it. I thought she might be heading for a ..."

"Liaison?"

"Right. And I was inclined to give it up then. But, since you did say all of those women could be in danger and as I'd already come this far, I decided to keep on a little longer and see what developed."

"And what did, Cousin?" Lydia asked. She gripped my arm a little tighter in her excitement and I wasn't about to object. Truth be told, I was just as curious, knowing Gutshall wouldn't be telling us this if Lizzie had simply been meeting a customer.

"Well," Gutshall said, and I detected a hint of excitement in the tone of his voice as he went on with his narration, "she led me clear to the other side of town. She ventured into an alley behind that tavern—the one called the *Bag O' Nails*."

"I know the one. Beiler's place."

"The very one," he said, nodding. "Anyway, I couldn't get too close without giving myself away. I crept as near I could and I discovered she was talking to someone. A man by the timbre of the voice, though I couldn't make out a word that was said."

"Could they have been..."

"No. They weren't together long enough and they left separately. I couldn't make up my mind should I follow him or her when they parted. I still feared for her safety, but I was curious about his identity. The man saved me the bother of deciding. As Lizzie walked away, the man came flying out of the alley on horseback. Since I was afoot there was no way I could follow him."

"And the girl?" Lydia asked.

"She came straight back home. Who do you think she might have been meeting and why, Tilghman?"

"That's what I'll be asking directly," I told him.

****

This proved more difficult than expected.

"Gone? What do you mean?"

"Just what I said," Matilda told me. "Packed her bag and left this morning without a word of explanation."

"Well where do you think she went?"

"She didn't tell either of us," Barbara said. "I think it's all my fault." I saw tears brimming in the girl's eyes. She sighed heavily and plopped down on the bench by the backdoor of the boarding house.

Tillie and I both glanced at her. "What does that mean?" I asked.

Barbara sighed again and dabbed at her eyes with an edge of her apron. "We had a fight last night. She snuck out after we went to bed. I heard her go and I was afraid. I waited up until she came back. She wouldn't tell me where she went and we had a row."

"A customer I didn't know about?" Matilda asked.

"No," Barbara said, shaking her head. "Nothing like that. She would have said if that were the case. This was something secret and she didn't like me prying. She never got mad at me like that before."

"Humph," Matilda said and she scowled.

"What?"

The woman stood with her hands on her hips and grunted again.

"Do you have an idea where she went?"

"He probably promised her more money, that's what."

"Who?"

Matilda swung her head toward me and her expression read like I was the dumbest man in creation. "Beiler. Who'd you think? She worked for him before and he's been tempting her to come back."

"Oh, I don't think so," Barbara said. "That's a bad place. She said she never wanted to go back there. She was treated badly by some men and..."

"Money compensates for a lot, girl," Matilda said, gruffly.

****

Between bouts of sneezing and nose-blowing, I spent the rest of my day searching for the girl. I might as well have saved my time for some other purpose. She was not to be found.

"Told you I haven't seen her," Beiler grumbled on my second visit to his establishment that afternoon. He dried his hands on a towel, flung it down and tapped himself a beer. "You want one?"

I was dry and I like an occasional beer as much as another man. But I wasn't inclined to patronize him. Leaning across the bar, I went eye to eye with the man. "I warn you, it wouldn't pleasure me to learn you were concealing knowledge of her whereabouts."

"I haint. I swear it." He backed away from me and took a swig from his mug. "If I knew where she was I'd tell you."

"She was seen outside this place last night, talking to a man."

"It weren't me. I haven't seen the girl in a good week. Last time was when I asked her to come back to work for me. Trade is better when they's a woman around—even if she haint the prettiest."

"If it wasn't you, do you have any idea who it might have been?"

Beiler shrugged. "How would I know? I was in here till closing—which was early last night. Business was lax. Afterward, I went straight upstairs to my bed. You could ask my woman—save I haint got one just now." And he guffawed at his effort at humor.

I didn't join him. I wasn't amused at the situation. And I was tired. Too tired to seek a meal with Lydia or others. My nose was sore and my head was stuffed up. I went straight home.

There I opened a tin of sardines and consumed them with a chunk of bread. Following my brief, solitary meal I sat in my rocker in the kitchen, intending to read the newspaper, a pursuit sorely neglected in recent days. I'd barely skimmed the headlines of the front page when I dozed off.

Had I lacked an observant friend that nap may have proven permanent.

OCTOBER 14, 1897

CHAPTER 17

I jolted upright in my chair, not sure what had awoke me. A noise? A chunk of wood burning through in the stove? Or was it the turning of the latch or a scraping at the door? I tried to rise, then sank back in my chair. My head was pounding, my throat dry and scratchy. And my stomach was in turmoil. I closed my eyes and succumbed to darkness and slumber.

Bright sunlight flooded through the window when I woke again. There was noise behind me, a drumming that didn't register at first. The door? There was someone pounding at the door. I rose, staggered across the room on unsteady feet. My head throbbed and my stomach was still queasy. I flung open the door.

"Sylvester," Hiram Mariner said, coming in. "Thank God you're all right."

I rubbed a hand across my face and stepped back to allow him entry. "Why wouldn't I be? Just a cold. Fell asleep in my chair. Got a bugger of a headache."

Mariner gripped me by the shoulders and directed me back to my chair. "Be glad that's all. Lord, if I'd known..."

I gazed up at him, quizzically. "Known? Known what?"

Doc bent over, checking my eyes, asking me to stick out my tongue, taking my pulse. "What in blazes is going on?" I asked, struggling to get up again.

"Sit a minute while I get some air in here." He'd left the door standing wide open and now he went around flinging up windows and letting cold air flow into the room. After a moment he came back and knelt by my side. "I should have checked on you last night. Are you feeling any better?"

Breathing in the frigid air, my head did seem clearer and my stomach less convulsive. "I don't understand. Why all the fuss? I have a cold and I fell asleep in my chair, but...wait a minute! Was it my stove? Was I asphyxiated?" I glanced, apprehensively, at my cook stove. I didn't remember lighting it last night, but if I had...

He looked at me and took my arm. "No. It wasn't carbon monoxide. Come outside a moment. I want to show you something."

Puzzled, I followed. Hiram pointed to my door. I followed his gaze and saw a thin length of tubing protruding from the keyhole. "What's that?"

Hiram scratched under his chin. He wore a hang-dog expression. "When I left the cat out last night I saw a man here at your backdoor. It was too dark to see who it was. When I called out to him, he ran off, went back through your yard and jumped the fence. I assumed it must have been a tramp, a prowler who didn't realize who lived here."

"What's that have to do..."

"When I didn't see you about this morning, I got worried."

"What time is it?"

"Late. Nearly eight o'clock. You're usually up and about, scrounging breakfast wherever you can by this time."

"Eight o'clock! I never sleep this late."

"It wasn't a natural sleep, my friend. When I didn't see you about I came over here. That's when I found that," he said, pointing to the tubing.

"What's it for?"

"Smell the end of the tube."

I took a whiff and jerked back. "Smells like medicine. What is it?"

"Chloroform. You must be getting too close to Runkle's killer. He inserted the tube through the keyhole and injected the anesthetic into the kitchen where he saw you asleep in your chair. He probably intended to enter and—I don't know? Slit your throat while you slept."

"Good grief. If you hadn't scared him off."

"Fortunately he didn't return to finish the task."

The thought gave me the shivers. I folded my arms around myself and gave him a grateful look. "Thanks, Hiram. I owe you..."

He clapped me on the shoulder. "I'm just glad you're all right. Look, here's what I want you to do. Let the door and windows open until the smell dissipates. Go wash up. I'll send one of the girls over with some broth. You eat that and when you feel better come over to the house. I have some news you've been wanting to hear."

"About the arsenic?"

"Yes. Do as I say now. We'll get to the other matter in due time."

I washed and changed my clothes. When I came back down to the kitchen, Emma was there with a bowl of consommé. "Father says you're to drink it all. Here, come to the table."

She stood over me as I ate. I have to admit, Emma was a pretty sight that morning to a man who'd nearly had his throat cut. She works as a secretary/bookkeeper for one of our local lawyers and it was obvious from her dress she'd stopped on her way to the office. The girl wore a bluish-gray nobby jacket with large lapels and velveteen trim over a plaid skirt. A hat with a big bow topped off the outfit. Emma stepped close and laid a hand on my shoulder. "I hope it makes you feel better quick," she said.

Just then Lydia stepped through the open doorway. "Sylvester," she said.

The girls exchanged a look. Emma dropped her hand from my shoulder and scurried off to one side.

"Is your cold better?" Lydia asked, coming into the room. "I was worried when you didn't show up for supper last night. I thought I'd come and check on you, but I see you're doing just fine."

"Someone tried to kill Sylvester last night," Emma said, making for the door.

"What?"

"He'll tell you about it. Goodbye, Syl. Don't forget, father said you should eat all that broth." Emma darted away.

Lydia came and sat down next to me. "Is it true? Someone tried..."

"I'm okay. Thanks to Doc." I told her what had happened.

I'll be honest, the jealous expression I saw on Lydia's face that morning almost made it all worthwhile, for it assured me of her affections even if it didn't guarantee she'd ever consent to marry me.

We talked a bit longer, then she went off to open the store after I agreed to come for supper that night.

****

I didn't expect an enthusiastic welcome or a confession, but at least the minister wasn't there to interfere. Catherine let me in and took me back to the parlor where Verbena was drinking chocolate from a dainty German cup. She didn't offer me any or invite me to sit. I wasn't sure I wanted anything to drink or eat in that household anyway. "I'll get you some coffee, Sheriff," Catherine said and bustled off. I didn't wait for her to return before informing Verbena of Doc's findings.

"It proves nothing," Verbena said, with a toss of her head.

"A witness will testify you purchased flypapers out of season," I told her. "Your sister-in-law said she saw you soaking them in a basin to get out the arsenic."

She smiled up at me. "So? I'll admit that. It doesn't mean I used it to kill my husband." Verbena leaned back in her chair and gave me another coy smile. Despite the late hour she was still in a cambric gown and a silk robe. Both seemed a bit colorful for a woman supposedly in mourning.

Catherine had returned and was pouring coffee into two cups behind me.

"Doctor Mariner found traces of arsenic on one of your handkerchiefs, in an aperient mixture and in a bottle of glycerin."

A cup clattered to the floor and I turned to see Catherine slumped on the sofa, her face gone pale. "Arrest her," she croaked, "arrest her."

Verbena laughed, a cruel little warble. "I don't know about the laxative. That may have been Valentine's. He was always buying medicines of one kind or another." She glanced over at her sister-in-law. "You know that, Catherine. Truly you do. You saw it as well as I. I know you've never liked me. But I didn't kill my husband."

"How do you explain the other?" I asked.

Verbena sighed and shook her head. "If you knew anything about women, Sheriff, you wouldn't need to ask. I did soak the flypapers—as I told you. But I only wanted the arsenic as a complexion aid."

I didn't say anything but I was aware many women did use the poison in potions for cleansing the skin. Verbena had a creamy, clear complexion and the flesh of her long white neck was as smooth as her face. I doubted she had need of any such artificial aid, but there was no way I could prove it.

"So you see," she went on, "your charges have no foundation. I admit to having drawn out the arsenic from the flypapers, but my purpose was entirely innocent." She stretched out her legs before her, exposing a trim ankle. I turned my gaze back to Catherine who looked at me with pleading eyes. "I'm sorry," I told her.

Catherine accompanied me out to the porch. "Isn't there anything you can do?"

"I wish I could offer more hope. We have nothing concrete. All the evidence is circumstantial. It wouldn't hold up in court and I don't think the district attorney would even allow me to bring charges with what we've got."

Catherine's dejected expression was enough to break a hard man's heart. She stared down at her feet a moment. "He was such a fool. He wouldn't listen to me. I tried to tell him a girl like her was only interested in his money. Now she'll have it all."

"Maybe. I'm not ready to give up yet. Tell me, were they married long?"

She raised her head, a glimmer of hope reflected in her eyes. "They were married less than a year, and he'd only known her a few weeks when he proposed. Do you know how they met?"

"No. I was about to ask."

Catherine snorted. "You'll recall his predilection for nostrums. She was working in the local pharmacy. She beguiled him with her charms and before long he was going there more to see her than to buy medicines. I'm sure the witch knows as much about arsenic and such as a chemist."

"Was she from Dauphin County, the same as you and your brother?"

"I can't say for certain. I believe she did leave it slip one time she'd lived in Lancaster previously."

****

I'm not overly fond of sauerkraut but Mrs. Longlow insisted I take a second helping. She said it would help clear my head of any lingering fumes of the chloroform and would help with my cold besides. Lydia's mashed potatoes and a fair-sized chunk of pork compensated for having to eat the kraut.

"So you're no closer to arresting her?" asked Gutshall who'd also been invited to supper again.

"Unfortunately, no."

He paused eating, holding his fork aloft. "I saw her in town the other day with that preacher. They seem a cozy pair. She's a fair-looking girl who probably could have had her pick of men. I only saw her husband in his coffin but, given his age and appearance, I would guess it wasn't love inspired her to marry him."

"Indications are it wasn't a mutual romantic attraction," I agreed.

"The two of you," Lydia said, clucking her tongue. "Who are you to be judging the poor woman? Not all matches are founded on appearances you know."

Gutshall and I exchanged a look and grin.

"What about the other case?" he asked then. "Did you hear back from the detective agency?"

I grimaced. "That's another source of frustration. Casey wrote and said they had a photo of Potteiger but his agent has misplaced it. All he could provide was a description."

"Well at least you have something to go on."

"I fear it won't be much help," I said and recited from memory, "A man about thirty-two years in age, five feet seven or eight in height, slim built, fair complexion, dark hair and eyes, sometimes wears a mustache, no distinguishing scars or marks. That could describe half the men in the county."

Gutshall guffawed. "Good luck in picking him out from the crowd."

"Well, I'm sure Sylvester will find him," Lydia said, confidently.

I gave her a grateful nod.

Later as Gutshall and I walked out I asked where he was bound.

"I thought I'd check on the women at the boarding house before going back to the hotel. How about you?"

"I intend to make up for last night's discomfort. A rocking chair isn't the best choice of a bed."

"You wouldn't want to go for a drink, would you?"

"Not tonight. Can you give me a rain check?"

"Sure. It's just—well, I was going to ask your advice about something."

"Oh? What might that be?"

He paused and turned to face me. In the dim light I saw he bore a boyish smile. "I met somebody. Lydia tells me she's a friend of yours and I thought—you know, man to man, you might..."

"What? Who are you talking about?"

"Her name is Emma Mariner. She works for that lawyer representing Mrs. Deibert."

OCTOBER 15, 1897

CHAPTER 18

I wasn't particularly thrilled about Gutshall paying court to Emma Mariner, but there wasn't much I could do about it if she was willing. Besides, him bringing up the subject had reminded me of something I'd thought about doing yesterday when Emma brought me the soup. I guess my brain was still a bit fogged at the time and that's why it slipped my mind.

Emma greeted me friendly when I arrived at the office and, though I didn't have an appointment, she beckoned me into her boss's office right after informing him I was there.

"Come on in, Sheriff," Darius Berkheimer said and indicated a chair before his big teak desk. "What can I do for you?" A heavy-set, stoop-shouldered man with sandy hair and a thick goatee, he regarded me closely with his small dark eyes. Though he was one of the most prosperous men in town and his political ambitions were being stoked by the big county powers, I'd never seen him without a frown.

"I was hoping you might answer some questions about the Deibert will," I said, taking the offered seat.

Berkheimer steepled his hands before him and shook his head. "You know I can't breach client confidentiality." Despite his size, the man had a shrill nasally voice and I didn't think much of him as a courtroom orator. He made most of his income in realty transfers, estate settlements and corporate dealings.

"Your client's dead."

"His wife is still my client."

"My questions pertain to him, not her."

"Ah, but she has informed me you see her as a suspect in her husband's alleged murder. Anything I say in regard to him might have impact on her situation should you decide to arraign her."

Giving him a sly look and a nod of my own, I said, "You want to get that spot in the district attorney's office I hear you covet it might be wise to disassociate yourself from the case. No harm in doing the probate work, but I don't think..."

That got his attention. Berkheimer narrowed his eyes and squinted at me. He fingered his beard a moment and gave me another nod. "Can anything we discuss be off the record?"

"Depends on what you tell me. For the time being I don't see any problem with that. Should it prove necessary to go otherwise, I'd be sure to inform you."

"All right. I'll listen to your questions and if I find them not harmful to Mrs. Deibert I'll answer."

"Fair enough. When did Valentine Deibert change his will?"

Berkheimer laughed. "Did Catherine Deibert put you up to this? You do know the fact Valentine left his money and property to Verbena does not leave Catherine out in the cold. The woman had a significant inheritance of her own from their parents. She's quite well off in her own right. That's why Valentine had no qualms about leaving her out of his will."

This was news to me. "I didn't know that. I thought the poor woman was destitute."

"I'm sure that's what she wanted you to think. She and Verbena don't get along. I'm sure you did realize that."

"Yes. I noticed. So, when did he change the will?"

"A week or so ago. I can get you the exact date if it's important to you."

"Not vitally so."

"It really wasn't that big an issue. Most of the estate would have gone to Verbena as a result of the original will I drew up when they first moved here. I suppose the poor man made the change out of guilt."

"Guilt? About what?"

"Why the baby, of course."

"What baby?"

"The one she lost. I think he took it harder than she did. And he blamed himself for getting her pregnant in the first place."

"I didn't realize they were married that long."

"Nearly a year. A long enough time."

"Why shouldn't a man get his wife pregnant?" I didn't see why that should be an issue. "That's what most married couples want, isn't it? I can understand him—and her—being upset if they lost the child. But..."

Berkheimer's frown worked itself deeper. "You didn't know, did you?"

"What? I don't understand."

He bobbed his head. "Of course you don't. Why should you be aware of a thing like that? I wouldn't have known had he not confided in me as his friend and legal advisor. What I'm about to tell you must be kept in the strictest confidence. Do I have your word?"

I was so eager to know—like an old woman seeking juicy gossip—I promised, though I wasn't certain I would keep my word.

"When they married," Berkheimer told me, "Valentine promised—presumably because of the age difference between them—that his and Verbena's marriage would be always a platonic affair. He thought at the time he would be satisfied with just having her beside him and being able to care for her. No normal man can keep such a promise. It's unnatural to think it could be done. Being in the presence of a woman one finds attractive and desirable inevitably leads to lust. Valentine, being human, succumbed to temptation on just one occasion. The result was Verbena became pregnant."

"And then she lost the child."

He bobbed his head again. "It proved too much for Valentine's conscience. The thought of what he had brought on her and himself weighed on him. Along with all his physical problems it contributed to his decline. He was very depressed toward the last. In fact, it wouldn't surprise me to learn he made this final financial gesture and then took his own life."

"You think he may have taken the arsenic himself?"

"I do."

****

From Berkheimer's office I went across the street to the pharmacy, hoping I might find there had been a minimal number of purchasers of chloroform in recent days and it would help me identify my attacker. This proved a waste of time. Anyone with a quarter can buy the stuff over the counter. Before ether, its invention had proved a blessing to the medical profession and their patients. Since then people have discovered a multitude of other uses for the compound—everything from a means of cleaning their carpets to a method of quelling bees in their hives. It's not common here in the country but I've heard there are people in the cities who've taken to inhaling it or even drinking it for a cheap drunk, though I can't imagine why anyone would find deranging their brain pleasurable. People do some odd things.

As I came out I saw a familiar figure glance at me and then scurry round the corner. I hustled after him and caught up with young Kintzler. "Were you trying to avoid me, Christopher?"

"Nah," he said, giving me a sheepish look. "Why'd you think that?"

"You took off soon as you spied me."

"No I didn't. Just in a hurry is all."

"I thought you didn't come in town?"

He colored and bent his head, mumbling into his coat.

"Say what?"

His eyes came up to meet mine. "Don't come in unless I have to. Any law against that?"

"None at all. You're a free man."

"Yeah." He spat off to the side, turned on his heel and continued down the alley.

I watched him out of sight then went back out to Market Street. Since it was nearing lunch time I decided to go by Mariners and see if I could get an invitation. I hadn't filled Hiram in on my confrontation with Verbena and considered that might be a valid excuse for turning up at his door. My real reason, of course, was to assess Emma's impression of Cyrus Gutshall. I didn't want to bring up the subject at her work and thought I'd do so as I walked her back to the office after lunch.

I got my invitation. Unfortunately, Emma didn't come home for lunch. Sissy said she was meeting a friend in town. I feared the friend might be Gutshall. Of course it wasn't my business. But I like the girl and I'm not thrilled about him.

"You didn't expect her to confess, did you?" Hiram asked after lunch as we had a cigar in his study. Though Doc is vehemently against cigarette smoking he regards an occasional cigar as therapeutic and an aid to contemplation. I'm less inclined to like them, but when you're a guest in another man's house you bow to his eccentricities.

"No, but I thought it might rattle her more than it did."

Hiram smiled. "The girl is definitely tougher than appearances might lead one to expect." He puffed pensively on his cigar a moment, then exhaled a cloud of blue smoke toward the ceiling. "Why the way she popped back after her miscarriage, that..."

I looked at him, startled. "You knew about it?"

"Why shouldn't I," he said, wrinkling his forehead and giving me a curious glance. "I am her physician."

"I thought they stopped coming to you?"

"Valentine did. She and Catherine remain my patients. But how did you know about her losing the child?"

I hesitated, taking a drag on my smoke. "A confidential source."

"Oh, he said—Catherine."

I didn't reply. If that supposition satisfied him I could keep my word to Berkheimer. After another puff of my cigar, I said, "I've been told theirs was meant to be a platonic marriage."

"So I was informed as well. Not that I believe it. There may have been less sex than in most normal marriages, but to imagine there was none..."

This conversation was getting a bit embarrassing for me. Still I was curious. "You think they did have relations—like other folks?"

"Given his corpulence and other physical limitations, Valentine may have been less inclined than most men. He was also more naïve about the subject than she. Certain things she said led me to believe she was not inexperienced when they married and had a healthy outlook on physical matters."

"You mean she was cuckolding him?" I asked, stunned.

Mariner laughed. "Oh, I wouldn't go so far as to say that. I simply meant she was capable and willing even if he was disinclined or physically limited."

I don't know if Hiram noticed but I believe I reddened as I contemplated the difference in their sizes and wondered how they might ever have accomplished the act. Sometimes it's best not to let curiosity take imagination too far.

****

"Your girlfriend was just in here looking for you," Lydia said when I stopped by the store.

"Barbara Frey?" I asked, thinking she might have some word of Lizzie.

"Oh, I forgot you have more than one. No. I was referring to Miss Mariner," Lydia said with a smug expression.

"Emma. Drat. I wanted to talk to her, too." I pulled out my watch and checked the time. "She's probably gone back to work now." Then, noticing the way Lydia was looking at me, I added, "She probably wanted to talk about Cyrus."

"Cyrus? What's he have to do with it?"

"Your cousin is seeing her. Last night he asked me to intercede with her on his behalf."

"Really?" Her face brightened with a smile. "That's wonderful. How long has this been going on? I wonder why he didn't tell me anything about it. And, you...why haven't you told me?"

"Whoa, girl. I just found out myself. Besides, it's none of our business if..."

"Why of course it is. Don't you see? If Cyrus is interested in this girl he'll be more inclined to stay here. And, that being the case, he'll be more interesting in accepting the job as your deputy. And she's a perfectly sweet and acceptable girl. This is just so wonderful!"

I was less inclined than she to be enthusiastic on either account. But at least it seemed it might win me some points with Lydia.

OCTOBER 16, 1897

CHAPTER 19

I didn't catch up to Emma until later that night. By then it was already too late. Lydia had taken the initiative and arranged a supper for the four of us (with her parents serving as chaperones who could be conveniently sent off to bed early). Emma, Cyrus and, especially, Lydia seemed pleased with the arrangement. I was a bit more dubious.

As usual, the supper part suited me just fine. Lydia had gone out of her way to prepare a special meal and, as always, her cooking was wonderful. We started with beef soup, followed by halibut with a parsley sauce. The main course was roast beef with potatoes and string beans. For dessert she had a lemon pie and there was plenty of coffee to wash it all down. I was stuffed when we left the table.

Five minutes later I was primed to go home but couldn't see any way of extricating myself from the company without upsetting the delicate balance of my relationship with Lydia. So I was obligated to sit there and keep my mouth shut and my opinions to myself for a half hour while Gutshall regaled us with another tale of his adventures in the west.

"Once when I was off hunting by myself in the mountains I got caught in a blizzard," Gutshall said. "I knew if I didn't find some shelter quick, I'd freeze to death. I sure didn't want that."

"So what did you do?" Emma asked, her eyes shining with

admiration.

"I found me a hollow tree, climbed inside and stopped up the opening with my blanket held in place by some sticks and my rifle. Then I just waited out the storm."

"Weren't you cold?" asked Lydia.

"Sure," he said with a nod, "but I knew I had enough fat on me to stave it off for the time needed. When the storm ended, everywhere I looked it was white and unfamiliar. But I was confident I was woodsman enough to find my way home."

"How on earth did you accomplish that?"

Gutshall smiled. "See, here's something not everybody knows. Moss grows most on the northwest side of straight trees and the limbs are bigger and more numerous on the south side. The tops of pine trees usually lean to the south, too. So I didn't need no compass. Thus I knew exactly which way I had to go. I reached our camp just as my friends were setting out to look for me—though they didn't expect to find me alive."

How such pretty and intelligent girls could be beguiled by his blarney is beyond me, but they were, the two of them sitting there with eyes fixed on him and rapt in attention to the man's every word. If that wasn't bad enough, Lydia kept giving me looks and prodding me to join in laughing at his lame jokes and applauding his accounts of derring-do—not a one of which I believed. Finally the windbag exhausted this round of his repertoire and I thought I might excuse myself. Didn't he turn around then and propose that he and Lydia entertain us with some music.

Now I don't for a minute mind listening to Lydia singing and playing. But the sentimental ballads he selected for their programme was enough to make me sick. On top of that I was forced to smile and nod in agreement whenever Emma leaned over and opined how wonderful he was. I wished I could do like Lydia's parents and retire to my bed.

It just goes to prove how far a man will go for the woman he loves.

When the musicale was done, Gutshall suggested we play a round of dominoes before calling it a night. Despite my objection it was getting late, the girls eagerly agreed. Lydia brought out the box and we went to the kitchen table to play.

Lydia dumped the box and spread the pieces. We each drew one. Gutshall and Lydia picked the high pieces, which partnered them against Emma and me.

Being chivalrous, Gutshall directed Lydia to lay down the first piece, which was a trois-blanc. Naturally, he was able to match her and she followed him again. He had to say "go" on the next round and Emma got in with a double-deuce. I didn't have a thing in my seven pieces, so I had to give the liberty to Lydia. Usually I'm a skilled player but this night I didn't have the strict attention the game requires and we went down to defeat quickly, earning me a scowl from my fair partner.

Lydia proposed another game. I was grateful when Emma said it was getting late and we all had to get up for church in the morning. Gutshall said he would walk her home. I took some of the wind out of his sails by saying it wouldn't be necessary since I was going in the same direction as her. "Well you can both walk me home," said Emma with a pleasant smile. "A wonderful idea," Lydia agreed. "A girl can never have too many escorts."

I was sullen as we walked and they chattered on like a pair of school children. Never was I so glad to see my house loom up before me as I was that night.

OCTOBER 18, 1897

CHAPTER 20

I'd been tied up in county court a good part of the day and the sun was already descending behind the western range of hills when I got back to Arahpot. Though it had been criminal court, none of the cases stemming from my jurisdiction had been major. Still they required my presence and I had to wait my turn to testify as the judge waded through the roster of cases on the docket.

It had been a dreary, windy day and there was a nip to the air, threatening frost overnight. The wind shuffled fallen leaves across our path and made my horse skittish. I was glad to be back home and away from the hustle and bustle of the county seat. My happiness increased when I noted a light still on in Lydia's store. I tied up and was on the sidewalk and about to enter when the door opened and Lydia and Gutshall came out.

"Sylvester," my love called out. "Did you have a good day?"

"A long one," I replied.

"Have you eaten?"

"Not yet."

"Well, I'm sorry, but you'll have to fend for yourself tonight. I'm off to a temperance meeting and I fear it'll be a long one."

That took the joy I'd momentarily held out of me.

"No problem," Gutshall said, coming over and clapping me on the shoulder. "He gave me a rain-check before on a supper at my hotel. Now's a good opportunity to cash it in."

I would have refused, but before I could get the words out, Lydia said, "What a wonderful idea. Have a good time, boys." And she went off, leaving me to face her cousin.

"So, what do you say? The hotel's right around the corner."

Grappling for an excuse, I asked, "What about Emma? Aren't you seeing her tonight?"

He gave me a boyish grin. "She's off to that same meeting with Lydia."

I didn't see how I could avoid it now. I figured I could abide the man's company long enough for the meal, then I'd make the excuse of being tired and go home.

The food at Tyler's Hotel isn't bad, though it's not up to the quality of what I usually enjoy at Lydia's or the Mariner's. Still I wasn't paying for it. We had a platter of fried oysters, potatoes and hard-boiled eggs and shared a pitcher of beer. Gutshall appeared to be as hungry as me and that kept conversation at a minimum.

We were finishing up our meal when our attention was attracted by a ruckus near the front door.

"What's going on here?" I asked, striding up to Bill Dunn, the manager, who had Harvey Ely by the lapels.

"Glad you're here, Sheriff," Dunn said. "I caught me a thief."

"That true, Harvey?"

Ely broke free from Dunn and hung his head, mumbling.

"Speak up, man."

"He tried to sneak out of here with a cup under his coat," Dunn said. "Might of got away with it but it fell and smashed on the floor. See, there," and he pointed to shards of china on the floor by the door.

Ely raised his eyes and looked at me. "Told him I'd pay for it. Only I don't have the money now." He hung his head again. I stood close enough to smell the booze on his breath. I grunted. Ely was a decent young man. He'd worked for the railroad until an accident last spring deprived him of an arm. Now he was reduced to what ever odd jobs he could find to support him, his wife and a baby. "What did you want with the cup, Harvey?"

He gave me a quick glance. "Thought it was pretty and might cheer Lois if I gave it to her."

"You think your wife would appreciate stolen goods?"

"I'd bought it I had the money."

"Are you going to arrest him, Tilghman? I'm ready to press charges."

I turned back to Dunn. "How much is that old tea cup worth, Bill?"

He shrugged. "I don't know. Maybe sixty-five cents."

I scowled at him. "How much?"

He grimaced and shrugged again. "We buy them in bulk. Set costs us maybe seven-forty-five."

"All right, here's what we're going to do. You get another one of those cups and give it to Harvey for his wife and you come up with an honest price what those two cups are worth. Harvey, you work off the value of those cups in whatever jobs Mister Dunn has for you."

"You're not going to arrest him?" Dunn asked.

"Would that pay for the cup got broke?"

"Well—no."

"Then you should see the virtue of my solution."

After a little more haggling, Dunn and Ely came to an agreement and Gutshall and I left the hotel.

"That was amazing," Gutshall said. "You were like Solomon resolving the argument between the two women. Most sheriffs would have just thrown the man in jail."

"Sometimes you just have to decide what's best for all concerned." I made my excuses and prepared to leave the man.

He said he needed to walk off his meal, so he'd accompany me back to where I'd left my rig. "How come you didn't join us in church yesterday?" he asked as we walked.

"Had paper work to catch up on. Figured if I didn't do it then, it wouldn't get done with court this week."

"You have to go back again tomorrow?"

"Yeah. Still one of my cases on the docket."

He glanced over at me. "Leaves the town unprotected, doesn't it?"

"That's why I'm still looking for a deputy." I was fearful he'd jump right in and ask for the job then. But he didn't.

"Too bad you didn't make it to church. Lydia had a nice solo. You would have enjoyed it."

I was about to say how much I regretted not hearing her sing when someone called my name.

"Sheriff! Sheriff Tilghman."

A man came running toward us. When he got closer I recognized his face but couldn't place the name. He drew up in front of us, bent over, hands on knees and panting. "Sheriff," he managed between gulps for air, "you gotta come. They're gonna kill somebody you don't."

"Who? What are you talking about?"

"Down at Beiler's. It's Wes Graeff and young Kintzler. They got into a brawl. Wes pulled a gun. He's gonna shoot somebody you don't stop 'em."

Cyrus looked at me. "I'll come with you."

I didn't argue. The three of us headed back to the *Bag O' Nails* fast as we could. On the way our informant told us what he had witnessed. "I don't know what started it. First thing I knew I heard raised voices. When I looked I saw Christopher with a big knife in his hand. Wes pulled out one of those little self-cocking revolvers. It must have caught on his pocket and it went off. Thank God, it didn't hit nobody. But he got real agitated then and started threatening anybody who wanted to interfere. Said he was going to kill Kintzler and nobody was gonna stop him. I was closest to the door. So I snuck out and come for you."

The situation was no better when we arrived at the tavern. Graeff, who I knew to be a hot-head, and Kintzler faced one another at the far end of the bar, the former waving his pistol around, and the latter brandishing a knife. Beiler's customers skulked against the far wall while the owner stood white-faced and wringing his hands behind the bar. "Come on, boys," he whined. "Give it up before you get in trouble."

"They're already in trouble," I said, striding toward the two antagonists. "Put the weapons down. Now!" Out of the corner of my eye I saw Cyrus jump the bar.

Graeff whirled toward me. "Get out of here, Tilghman. This haint your business."

He was distracted just long enough for Kintzler to lunge at him with the knife. Graeff swung back and pointed the pistol at the other's chest. "Keep away. I'm warning you. I will shoot."

It was just then that Gutshall who had crept down along the bar leaped over it, kicking Graeff on the shoulder. The gunman staggered back but his weapon went off, the bullet cutting a furrow across the top of Kintzler's hat. The young man jumped backward, dropping his knife. As Graeff spun back toward Cyrus I jumped him and wrestled the weapon from him.

Gutshall whistled between his teeth. "Thanks. He might have shot me."

"If you pulled foolish stunts like that out west it's a wonder you made it back here alive."

He gave me a chastened grin.

"Grab hold of that other one and help me cart them down to my jail," I said. "Oh, and don't forget the weapons."

****

I put the two of them in separate cells, thanked Gutshall for his help and sent him home. Then I went back to talk to Kintzler.

"Didn't expect to be back in no cell so quick," he said, giving me a pathetic look. Even the plainest men have their touches of vanity. Though he was dressed like any common farmer, Christopher Kintzler displayed his in the plug hat he wore (now ruined by a bullet hole) and a navy blue with white polka dot muffler knotted round his scrawny neck.

"Lucky you're not dead. What brought this on? I thought you kept out of town."

He sat down on the bunk and looked up at me. "I don't like coming into town. But that one owes Pa some money and he won't pay. I came to collect and he pulled that gun on me." He removed his hat and laid it on the bunk beside him.

"He drew the knife first," came Graeff's voice from the next cell.

"Doesn't matter who drew first," I told him. "I don't take kindly to people threatening others with harm in my town. Why didn't you pay Ollie what you owe him?"

"Cause he didn't do what he promised."

"You knew right from the start there couldn't be no guarantee," Kintzler countered. "Maybe you didn't do as he told you. Sometimes a little thing can make it not work."

"My little girl's sick," Graeff said to me. "He promised to make her better and he didn't. Why should I pay for what don't work?"

"You contract for a service, you're supposed to pay," Kintzler said. "Pa always does his best. But it don't always work. That's just the way it is."

"You got any money, Wes?" I asked him.

He shook his head. "No. I didn't have the money to go to Doc Mariner. That's why I went to Kintzler. He's cheaper. I figured if it worked, I'd find some way to pay him. But it didn't work and I don't have no money to pay anyhow."

I leaned against the bars and shook my head. "I want the two of you to listen. I could just keep you in here over night, then bail you out at $300 a head pending a hearing before Squire Fegley."

"I haint got..." they said almost in unison.

"Shut up and listen! I said I could do that. But the main thing at concern here is a little girl who's sick. Now if you had any sense at all, Wes, you would have gone to Doc and explained your situation. That's what I want you to do in the morning. Doc Mariner puts people and their needs above money. He will help your little girl as much as he's able. You've put her in more jeopardy by hesitating to do that in the first place.

"Second, Christopher, next time you or your Dad need help in collecting a legitimate debt you come to me. You don't go threatening people with a knife. You hear?"

"Yes, sir."

"Now both of you get some sleep and be prepared to shake hands and act like human beings in the morning. Understood?"

"Yes, sir." Both of them said.

I was half way out the aisle when the two of them called me back. Wes wanted me to explain to his wife where he was and Kintzler wanted a similar message sent to his father. It looked like I wasn't getting to bed just yet.

OCTOBER 19, 1897

CHAPTER 21

My court duties were over early enough to get me home by late afternoon. I went directly to Doc Mariner's office. Fortunately he was clear of patients and I got to see him right away.

"Did Wes Graeff get his little girl in to see you?"

"He did," Hiram said with a nod, but his expression was solemn. "It would have been better if I'd seen her earlier."

"Is she going to be all right?"

"Time will tell," he said with a shrug. "Whooping cough. If they'd got her in to see me sooner...well, no use going on about that now. She's developed inflammation of the lungs. There could be convulsions. The child is in a weakened condition and the situation is dangerous. I've prescribed for her and I'll go out to the farm and check on her again tomorrow morning."

I shook my head, feeling sympathy for the child and anger at her father. "I told him he should have brought her here sooner. What is wrong with people? It's only common sense..."

"He told me it wasn't superstition took him to Kintzler. He was concerned about the cost of treatment. I've been doctoring here long enough people should know me. Well, nothing either of us can do about it. You up for a cup of coffee?"

"Thought you'd never offer."

He led me back to the kitchen where Clara and Sissy were busy rolling out dough for pot-pie. It gladdened my heart to see them rolling and cutting their own dough. There's a trend nowadays in many kitchens—even here—to use the ready-made stuff. Though she doesn't approve of it herself Lydia even carries the packages in her store. She says it's necessary to have available what customers want. I'll admit it's probably less work for women but how can stuff made in a factory compare with home-made?

Clara greeted me and asked if I'd eaten. I hadn't but figured I'd cadged enough meals from them lately and declined the offer. Hiram got our coffee and we retired to his study.

"Did you have a look at it?" I asked after we'd seated ourselves. I was referring to Kintzler's knife. Despite releasing the man and being sympathetic to his reason for drawing the weapon, I hadn't forgotten it or totally eliminated him as a suspect in Runkle's murder. I had Simon give the knife to Hiram before leaving for court.

"I did," he said. "The blade is large enough to have been the one used to stab Runkle. But I can't say for certain it was the one in question."

"That doesn't help me a bit."

"Sorry, but it's the best I can do."

"Was there blood on it?"

"None that I could make out. But it was cleaned recently."

I frowned. "Most country people keep their tools and weapons clean."

"Do you see this young man as your best suspect?"

"No. Not especially. I'd just like to find whoever is guilty. I owe it to this poor fellow who'd been cheated and came to our town in hope of justice. He got himself killed and somebody has to pay. What happened to his wife by the way? I haven't seen her around the last couple days."

"Clara wanted her to stay on longer. But the woman said she'd burdened us long enough and it was time she went back home. I guess she has some relatives and friends back in Lancaster County and she'll turn to them now."

"I wish I could have said goodbye and assured her I'm doing my best to find her husband's killer."

"She expressed appreciation for your efforts. Whether you find the killer or not, it won't bring back her husband."

That was true enough. Still I felt bad.

Hiram finished his coffee and sat aside the cup. "Did you find any evidence Kintzler was preceded here by his wife?"

"No. He claims she left him when he went to prison. Other than the incident last night I've found few people even knew he was here, let alone a wife. And I haven't found anybody else fits the bill of this mysterious Phoebus Potteiger. I wish I had a picture and knew what he looks like." I drained my cup and sat it next to Hiram's.

"You want anymore?" he asked, gesturing at the cups.

"No. I guess I should be getting back to the office." I started to get up.

"Can you answer me a question before you go?" he asked, an expression I couldn't quite interpret on his face.

"Sure. If I can," I told him, sitting back down.

"This fellow. This Gutshall that's been seeing Emma lately."

"Yes?"

"What do you think of him?"

The question put me in a quandary. I personally wasn't overly fond of the man and I didn't think he was a particularly good suitor for Emma. But, not knowing how she or her family felt about him, I didn't want to stir up any needless trouble. "He's Lydia's cousin. I'm not sure..."

Hiram leaned toward me, darted a glance toward the open door of the study and lowered the tone of his voice. "I think the man's a braggart," he said, "and I'm not overjoyed by his attentions to my daughter. He has the women of my household all a-flutter and Em seems to like him. But he's been in the army and that can warp a man's attitude toward a girl's virtue. Do you think he's trustworthy?"

"Honestly Hiram, I don't know. Gutshall has a way with the ladies for sure. Lydia thinks he walks on water. But, then, he is her blood. She's been trying to persuade me to hire him as deputy."

Mariner sat back and rubbed a hand across his face. He gave me a direct look. "Are you going to do it? If you did, a steady job might incline me to have a better opinion of the man."

I pursed my lips and thought a moment. Then I told him, "I'm not sure I like him for a deputy or a suitor for Emma."

Hiram bobbed his head. "Then I guess we're of one mind. I know he's been helping you out some. It'd be a relief to me if you occupied him more so he wouldn't have the time to infatuate my girl anymore than she already is."

Hiram's my friend, but I thought that was much to ask of a buddy.

****

A short time later, heading down the street, I ran afoul of Charlie Fegley and McLean Ruppenthal.

"Tilghman," Charley called, and by the look on both their faces I knew I was in trouble. Uh-oh. I stopped and awaited their approach. "What happened to the men you took in custody last night?"

"I let them go."

"So we heard," Ruppenthal said, a frown apt to break a mirror twisting his features. Mac is burgess of our borough and sometimes I think he believes the title equates with king. He's one of those nasty little men who given a little power do all they can to increase its scope. Some are inclined to say his nature is the result of mixing Irish and German blood. Personally I contend some people are just born mean. He practically stood now on tiptoe to stretch his height closer to my six-foot, his dark eyes nearly popping out of their sockets.

"Why'd you do a fool thing like that?" Charlie asked.

"I figured they'd learned their lesson."

"It's not your prerogative to decide that," Ruppenthal snapped.

"Do you want me to re-arrest them?"

"It's a little late for that," he said, jabbing a finger at me like it was a weapon. "This is just a warning, Tilghman. You can be replaced, you know." He glanced from me back to Charlie. "I've got to get to the store. You talk to him, Fegley." And he strode off. Ruppenthal owns the local haberdashery store. I try not to buy more than I have to in the place.

Charlie watched him go. Then he turned back to me. "You better watch your step, my friend. He don't like you." And he grinned.

"The feeling's mutual."

"Yeah. Well don't take him lightly. What's the matter with you anyhow? You know you should have brought those fellows before me for a hearing."

I nodded. "Ordinarily I would have. But it was just a misunderstanding. No one got hurt. And neither one has any money. Besides, I have more important things on my mind."

It was his turn to nod. "You any closer on those?"

I frowned. "Not as close as I'd like to be."

"Well, keep on it. But watch your step."

****

I picked up my mail and went back to the office to sort it, hoping for better news from the detective agency. Lydia was busy with a good crowd of customers and we only had a moment to talk. I did manage to get another supper invitation. It was good to have something to brighten my day.

The mail didn't. It was the usual pile of nothing. I was debating what to do next when my door popped open and a little boy stuck his head in. "Sheriff Tilghman?" he asked.

"That's me. What is it, boy?" I thought he looked vaguely familiar, but I couldn't quite place him.

"If you're the sheriff, I got a message for you," and he held out an envelope.

I took it and the boy scuttled off before I could ask any questions. I was sitting there holding the envelope and trying to remember where I'd seen the boy when Gutshall walked in. "Kid almost knocked me over," he said. "What's that you got there?"

"You're getting to be a real nuisance."

"Is that any way to talk to a friend?" he asked with a wide grin.

I wasn't inclined to give him the satisfaction of answering that one. "What is it you want, Gutshall?"

He sat on the edge of my desk and folded his arms across his chest. "I was just wondering if you'd happened to mention my virtues to Miss Mariner yet?"

"I've been busy," I said, curtly.

"Yeah. I know. But you do get over there. They are your neighbors, aren't they?"

"They are."

He had a boyish look despite his mustache and size as he sat there staring at me. "Syl, I'd be real grateful if you could talk to her. Emma is a real treat. I do like her and I'd want..."

"Her dad isn't exactly thrilled about you courting her," I blurted. I hadn't meant to tell the man that. It just came out.

Gutshall looked genuinely hurt now. "He said that?"

I nodded. "Said he wasn't comfortable about your intentions toward the girl."

"Oh, Lordy. My intentions are honorable. I'd never hurt..."

"I'm just telling you what he implied."

Cyrus took a deep breath and swallowed. He plucked at his mustache and stood up. "I got to go talk to him. I got to convince him..."

"He's of the opinion men who've been in the army are inclined to take advantage of women, to corrupt their morals."

"Oh, I'd never do that. Some might, but I'm not like that. I've got to go talk to the man." He headed for the door, then turned back. "I'll see you later tonight. At Lydia's. I'm coming for supper, too. You will talk to Em, won't you?" And he was gone.

I sat there a moment longer, wondering if he was sincere and really did care about Emma. Then I picked up the envelope and tore it open. It was brief and to the point:

I heared you wanted to talk to me. If you do meet me tonight in the alley behind your office at ten. I'll be there.
Lizzie

That was when I remembered where I'd seen the boy and who he was. He was Lizzie Kline's son. I'd seen him that day emptying the slop jar at Beiler's. At the time I didn't know who he was. It was later when I'd had second thoughts about the lad skipping school I reported him to Truant Officer Ritter.

"I know exactly which boy you're talking about," Ritter said. "He's that Kline girl's bastard. I've talked to her till I'm blue in the face. Don't do a lick of good. She told me she never had schooling and she's doing just fine. Said Nick don't need none either. The boy is better off working for his keep. Can you imagine a mother like that?"

"He's Lizzie's boy?"

Ritter nodded. "You know how it is with women like her. Sooner or later, they get pregnant. At least she decided to keep him. Most just solve the problem in other ways decent folk don't want to know about. You know what I mean?"

I did. It wasn't my business. Still I felt concern for the educational opportunities the boy was missing out on. "Do you think it'd do any good if I talked to her?"

He gave me a quizzical look. "Go ahead. No skin off my nose. I haint wasting no more of my time on them."

I was sincere about talking to Lizzie. Things got out of hand then and the opportunity never presented itself. I laid her note aside and scratched at my chin. Maybe after tonight I would broach the subject with her.

CHAPTER 22

I kept my plans to meet Lizzie to myself that night at supper. Lydia wouldn't approve of my meeting a girl like Elizabeth Kline in a back alley at night no matter what kind of sensible reason I offered for it. Better to just keep quiet on the subject. No one else at the table—her parents and Cyrus Gutshall—needed to know either. Gutshall had other concerns on his mind and kept asking if I'd had time to talk to Emma. I hadn't and I still wasn't sure I wanted to. But I couldn't bring myself to tell him so. He really had seemed hurt when I told him about Hiram's opinion of him.

"Sorry, Cyrus," I said after he asked about the second or third time. "I just didn't have time today. Maybe I'll get round to it tomorrow."

"I sure would appreciate that, Syl. It would mean a lot to me."

"What are you two gabbling about?" Lydia asked.

Before I could say anything Gutshall told her. "Doctor Mariner doesn't like the idea of me seeing Emma."

"Why on earth not?" Lydia asked. She shot a look at me. "What does he have against my cousin?"

I ducked my head down between my shoulders like a turtle. "I'm not sure. I think he has a bad impression of men who've been in the army."

"I was in the army and he's always been cordial to me," Lydia's father said.

"Yes, but you weren't interested in courting his daughter, Uncle," Cyrus said.

"Oh," the old man said with a sudden knowing look. "Oh." And he mouthed a grin that soon broke into a chuckle.

"Father," Lydia said, catching on. And she reddened a bit. "Cyrus isn't like that. He's a perfect gentleman and you know it. I can't imagine what Doctor Mariner might have against him. Besides Emma seems to have taken a strong liking to our cousin which has distracted her attention from our Sylvester."

Gutshall scorched me with a look now. "What does that mean? Is there something you haven't told me, Syl? Is that why you haven't talked to her?"

"No," I said, and it was my turn to blush. "There's only one woman I'm interested in," I told him, looking over at Lydia. "Just because we're neighbors and friends your cousin has taken it into her head there's more than that between us."

"No," Lydia said, jumping to her own defense and explaining to Gutshall, "I never implied Syl had any interest in Emma. But there's no denying the girl had a crush on him forever before you came along."

Gutshall brightened with this news. "So you really think I have a chance with her then?"

Lydia gave him a smile and a nod.

"Well that's great news," he said. "I'm got my appetite back now. Would you pass the potatoes, please?"

****

I made my excuses and got out of there as soon as I could. Lydia and Gutshall both wanted to play board games but I convinced them I was too tired from traveling back and forth to Shannon two days in a row for court and wouldn't be able to concentrate. I said after a good night's rest I'd be primed to compete on the morrow. Reluctantly, they gave in and I left.

My interest in what Lizzie might have to tell me had made me a poor guest that night anyway. My mind kept drifting and imagining scenarios and several times Lydia had to prod me to bring me out of a fog when she or one of the others engaged me in conversation.

I would have left sooner if it hadn't aroused their suspicion something was going on.

Time passed slowly that evening but finally it was approaching the hour Lizzie had set for our rendezvous. Again my mind was wandering and painting scenarios as I walked down the darkened streets of my town. I was anxious to ask who she'd met that night and why she ran away afterward.

Frost had crisped the leaves brought down by recent rains and they crackled underfoot. Save for the dismal honking of a flight of geese overhead, the shuffling of my feet through these leaves was the only sound. I glanced up and saw the vee of the geese silhouetted against a moonlit cloud. There was a lamp on the corner just before my office. Despite the chill in the air, Catocala moths (what we commonly call Birch moths) hovered in the glow of its light.

Looking up at the light blinded me momentarily and I hesitated before heading down the alley behind the building. It was black as pitch. I listened but heard not a sound. I took a step forward. "Lizzie?" I queried.

Silence.

I took another couple steps and called out again.

A figure stepped out from the side of the building in front of me. "Sheriff?"

"Lizzie. Is it you?" She was no more than a shadowy form in the gloom.

"Yeah," she said.

"Why'd you want to meet here? You could have just come to my office."

The girl stepped back away from me. I couldn't make out her features in the darkness.

A boot heel scraped on paving behind me and I started to turn.

A body flung against me and knocked me stumbling toward the wall. Lizzie screamed. Before I could recover the other figure whose identity I couldn't make out rushed toward me. "Don't. Please don't!" Lizzie cried. I saw the flash of something in the dim light as he raised an arm. Though I couldn't make out who I was certain it was a man. I swerved to the left as he came at me and his arm came down in an arc. Cloth ripped and I felt a sting to my right shoulder but I whirled around and aimed a kick at his shin.

My kick missed and my assailant backed off, circling round again. I saw his arm go up once more.

"Hey!" came a voice from the end of the alley.

My attacker spun round, seizing Lizzie who quailed against the far wall. She groaned as he flung her toward me. I tried to side-step but was too late. The girl careened into me and the two of us stumbled back and fell. He stepped toward us again. Then something whistled through the air. My assailant howled in pain and staggered back. He whirled and took off running into the dark. As I lifted Lizzie and tried to get up I heard the slap of footsteps hurrying toward us.

"Are you all right?" Cyrus Gutshall asked, bending over and extending a hand to me.

****

"You ought to be grateful," Cyrus grumbled. "I saved your life again."

I knew he probably had saved my life this night. But I wasn't quite ready to admit it with him standing over me and grinning while Doc Mariner tended the cut on my shoulder. "What do you mean, again?"

"You know—the other night at Beiler's. If I hadn't of jumped that fellow he would have shot you sure."

I wasn't ready to accept that one. Personally I thought he was the one most at risk in that incident. "How'd you know where to find me anyway?"

Gutshall blanched. "You gonna be mad?"

"Why would I be mad? Like you said, you following me probably saved my life."

"I came back to your office this afternoon. I was going to prevail on you..." He hesitated and glanced at Hiram. "Well, you know. You'd left that note laying on your desk."

"And you read it?" He was right. I was irked he had the audacity to read my personal mail. Still, under the circumstances, I was glad he did.

Gutshall nodded. "I knew what you were up to. I thought you might ask me to help. But you didn't. So I left Lydia's right after you and followed along. Good thing I did, too." And he grinned. "Instead of being sore at me you should be thankful."

"He's right," Hiram said as he finished dressing my injury. "This cut isn't serious. But your assailant could have inflicted much worse. This is the second time Potteiger tried to kill you. He might have succeeded this time if not for Gutshall here."

"You think it was him?"

"Don't you? I mean, who else has reason to want you dead? You must be getting too close to him for his comfort."

I nodded. "You're right. I believe it was him." I glanced over at the figure on the surgical table across the room. Lizzie hadn't been as fortunate as me. "What made you think I needed support when all I was doing was meeting a woman?" I asked Gutshall.

"I don't know. Maybe just a hunch. Couldn't figure why she wanted to meet in a back alley when she could have just come to your office. It wasn't like she'd committed no crime."

"Well, I'm glad you had that hunch." I could have kicked myself for not having as much sense. I'm the lawman. I should have had a premonition, too. I hadn't even bothered to carry my pistol or a nightstick. I looked over at him. "Cyrus."

"Yeah?"

"I am grateful."

He beamed another of those boyish grins.

"What was it you threw at him anyway?"

He gave a little laugh. "As I came in the alley I stumbled on a pile of loose bricks there at the corner. When I realized what was going on I picked one up and flung it at him. I think I hit him, too. Did you hear him cry out?"

"I did. I hope it struck him in a place where it'll leave a mark so I can pick him out of a crowd. I still don't have a clue what the bugger looks like." I felt a bit of a twinge as I shrugged into my jacket. This compelled another glance over at Lizzie's still form. "Do you think she suffered much, Hiram?"

The doctor shook his head, his eyes also going to the girl. "His thrust was sure this time. Under the rib cage and pierced her heart. She was probably gone before she hit the ground."

"She gave a little moan when he seized her but I thought it nothing but surprise at his action. The poor thing. I should have insisted she come to the office. Had I known..."

"You had no idea where to find her."

I wiped a hand across my face. "I could have tried. The boy—her son—he knew where she was."

"What of him now?"

"Do you think the lad is in danger, too?" Gutshall asked.

"I don't know. I'll have to find him and see to his protection." Another glance at Lizzie. "He'll have to be informed of his mother as well." I sighed.

"I'll go with you," Gutshall offered and this time I wasn't inclined to refuse.

"Be careful of that shoulder," Hiram said as he escorted us to the door. "Come back in the morning and I'll change the dressing. Don't want you getting no infection."

"How did you know which of us was which?" I asked Cyrus as we walked out to the street. "You might have hit me with that brick instead of him."

"Not likely," he said and chuckled. "Despite the dark I couldn't mistake the size of you for your assailant. He was at least a head or two shorter and not half so wide."

OCTOBER 20, 1897

CHAPTER 23

Belching steam and gasping like a dragon in labor, Engine Forty-three pulled up at the station, disgorging a few passengers. Wearing his blue uniform and hard cap, Ezra Weikel, the stationmaster, strode along the platform, bellowing the boarding call in stentorian tones. I watched as some locals and a scattering of others making the connection from other points streamed out of the station and climbed into the waiting cars. The train hissed and rumbled and the stack blew out sparks and cinders.

Checking my watch I turned to Weikel. "She's late."

"Only a bit," he said. "Conductor told me they had some cows on the tracks up the way. She'll make up the time going on to Shannon." Taking off his cap and rubbing a hand across his bald pate, he walked off.

I also had business to tend to. Coming down to watch the train come in had been a delaying tactic. The boy, Nick, awaited me at Matilda Rebuck's place. He had to be informed about his mother. Earlier I'd sent Simon Hinkle to find him after conferring with Barbara Frey and Matilda. As friends of his parent I hoped they'd help in consoling the lad. Still the task wasn't one I looked forward to undertaking.

As I started up the platform, the ticket agent called out to me.

"What do you need, Tom?" I asked going up to his window.

"Naught I need, Sheriff. I was just wondering if he found you."

"Who?"

"Why the man who was looking for you."

"What man? When?"

Tom gave me a look like I was dense. "Came in on the Forty-seven yesterday afternoon. Said he wondered where he might find you. I sent him up to your office. Didn't you see him?"

I shook my head. "Who was he?"

"Didn't give me his name, did he? How would I know?"

I wasn't expecting any visitors. But occasionally other lawmen or people having business with the law or searching for some missing person did stop in. "What did he look like?"

Tom squinted and pursed his lips. "Skinny fellow, red hair going gray, bushy side whiskers. Wore a cheap suit. That's the best I can remember."

I supposed the man might have changed his mind or delayed stopping in for one reason or another. Well, I had other business. If it was important and the fellow was still around he'd find me. I headed off to Matilda's.

****

Nick was a tough little fellow. He held out till near the end of my report before emotion took hold and his tears broke forth. Barbara cradled him in her arms and stroked his hair while Matilda sat in stony silence by her side.

I waited until the boy's crying wore down to an occasional snuffle. Then I asked if he knew where his mother had been since leaving Matilda's. He raised his tear-streaked face and snorted. I gave him my hanky and he blew his nose. "With me," he managed. "In my shed."

"Your shed?"

"Beiler makes the boy sleep in a little lean-to at the back of the tavern," Barbara said. "It's where we found him this morning. The place is hardly big enough for the likes of him. I don't know how the two of them squeezed in there." She hugged the boy close as his tears started afresh.

"Did anyone come to see her while she was with you?"

Nick raised his head and shook it.

"All right." I stood up, prepared to leave. "I may want to talk to you again later, Nick. Is that okay?"

The boy nodded, then buried his head against Barbara's breast.

"What's to become of the lad?" I asked. "Did Lizzie have any family around here?"

"None," Barbara said. "Her parents were gone long ago and I don't think she had any brothers or sisters. There's no one."

"That's what orphanages are for," Matilda said.

"Mother!" Barbara cried, giving her a discerning glance.

Mother?

"That's right," Matilda said, looking up at me. "This one's my daughter."

"But your name..."

"Is different." She shrugged. "So I was married a couple times."

I was surprised, but I wasn't going to get into why a mother would have her daughter involved in the kind of life Barbara and Elizabeth lived. It wasn't for me to judge them.

"And Nick isn't going to no orphanage," Barbara said, firmly. "And he's not going back to Beiler's either."

"We can't..." Matilda started.

"Yes we can, Mother. And we will. We owe that much to Lizzie."

Gratified by the girl's spunk, I turned to leave.

"Nobody came to see her," Nick said, suddenly, "but she went out a couple times."

I turned back. "She did?"

The boy nodded. "Told me she had to see a man. I think she was scared of him. Once she said he wanted her to do something she didn't want to do. Was he the one killed her?"

Was being a decoy to bring me to him what she didn't want to do? "I believe so, Nick. And I promise you, I'm going to do everything I can to find and punish him."

****

I went back to my office, pondering should I go and see Beiler again. The man must have known where Lizzie was when he told me he didn't. Could he know anything more about who it was made her his pawn and then killed her?

I was seated at my desk thinking these thoughts when Simon Hinkle showed up bearing a lunch basket.

"Doctor Mariner said I should see if you wanted me to run any more errands," the boy said, setting the basket before me. "And Mrs. Mariner thought you might be needing some lunch."

Gratefully, I opened the basket. "I don't have any tasks for you right now, Simon. Have you eaten? You want to share this with me?" I dug out the contents. There was cold veal, nicely sliced. Bread, butter, pickles, a chunk of cheese and a baked potato. In a separate container I found a good-sized piece of chocolate cake with thick, creamy frosting. Clara hadn't sent a beverage, but she knew I always had coffee.

"I already ate," Simon said, "but I wouldn't mind a piece of that cake." He pulled up a chair next to the desk.

Simon gobbled up more of the cake than I might have preferred. But I couldn't object. The boy did me plenty of favors and he was a growing lad with a bounteous appetite. I didn't begrudge him my sweets.

"Did he catch up with you?" Simon asked at length, licking frosting from a thumb.

"Who?"

"That man was looking for you."

"When?"

"Yesterday. He came up from the station. Must have come in on Forty-seven. I'd come by to see if you needed me and found him peering in the window."

The man Tom had mentioned. "Did he say who he was? What he wanted?"

The boy looked up at me. "No. I didn't know then you'd gone to Shannon for court. I told him you'd probably be in the office later. The man said he intended on checking into the hotel and would come back after. Didn't he?"

I wagged my head. "Must have missed him. When I'm finished here I'll go over to the hotel and see if he's still around or if he left a message for me."

****

But at the hotel I learned the man wasn't there. "He got your message and went off," the clerk told me.

"What message? I sent no message."

The clerk shrugged. "He was no sooner up in his room than a boy came with an envelope for the man. The lad said it was from Sheriff Tilghman and it was urgent. So I had it taken right up. The guest came right down and checked out."

"Did this guest have a name?"

"Of course. Mister Reilly," the clerk said with an officious smile.

"Do you know where this Mister Reilly came from or what his business with me might have been?"

"I have no idea where he came from. He sent a telegram ahead, reserving a room. He didn't inform me of his business, sir, and I didn't ask."

OCTOBER 21, 1897

CHAPTER 24

"How's your shoulder?" Lydia asked.

"It still stings a bit when I move, but Doc says it's healing nicely. I guess I'm lucky the blade didn't slice any deeper than it did."

"And that Cyrus was there. I shudder to think what might have happened had he not come along."

I wasn't quite ready to admit it out-loud, but I was grateful the man had followed me. He'd become even more obnoxious now and prone to telling everyone met how he'd saved my life. It wasn't something I liked. Lydia and Emma fawned over him even more than in the past and it sickened me. Yet I had no choice save to abide it.

I'd stopped by the store on the pretense of wanting to check my mail but actually for an opportunity to have Lydia to myself, a goal seldom achieved of late. Cyrus Gutshall and Emma Mariner had become like appendages in recent days.

I'd come by the store following another confrontation with that other irritating personage, Jake Beiler.

"I give the boy a place to sleep," he'd snarled, "I don't tuck him in at night."

"Then you're telling me once more you didn't know Lizzie was back there?"

"I did not. How many times do I have to say it?"

"I don't believe you, Beiler, and I'm going to continue asking questions."

He sneered. "You can harass me all you like. I've told you what's so."

Much as I believed Beiler knew more than he was telling me I had no means to shake it out of him. The man could rest assured I'd be keeping a close watch on all his activities in future.

I'd also asked Nick if he was the boy delivered the message to Reilly. The lad seemed not to know what I was talking about. So that was another puzzle to gnaw on. There were plenty of young boys in town who would gladly run errands for a little change. No way I could interview them all to find the right one.

"You're looking deep in thought," Lydia said now, returning my attention to the present.

I sat on a plank-bottomed chair and propped my feet up on the fender of the potbellied stove. With my hands cradling the back of my head I gazed up at her. "Three murders and I'm no closer to solving any of them than I was a week ago."

She gave me a warm smile and reached out to touch my arm. "You'll get to the bottom of it."

"I wish I was so confident. I'm convinced Verena Deibert poisoned her husband and I can't find the proof I need to arrest her. I haven't an idea who this Phoebus Potteiger is or where to find him. And now Ruppenthal is on my back. If something doesn't happen soon I may have to quit this job."

Lydia had walked over to the counter for some purpose. She whirled around now, facing me. "Don't you dare give up, Sylvester Tilghman. You are good at your job and everyone knows it—even McLean Ruppenthal. I know you. You will keep on digging, picking away like a child at a scab, until you uncover the answers required. So I don't want to hear any more talk of you quitting."

I lowered my head, unable, unwilling to meet her steady gaze.

Hearing the rustle of her skirts, I lifted my head. Lydia knelt beside me and took my hands in hers. "I believe in you," she said, quietly.

How could I give up in the face of such confidence?

She brought some cold chicken and ham sandwiches and sat them before me. "You'll feel better with some nourishment."

Gratefully, I ate.

"Do you really think Verbena did it?" she asked as she sorted mail behind the counter.

"I'm inclined to think so."

"She seems so quiet and docile. Not at all like the sister-in-law."

I smiled. "Catherine takes some getting used to. Appearances are deceiving, you know. She's not so bad as you think. And what the woman told me of how Verbena and her brother came to marry and what I've learned of their relationship together makes me even more suspicious her goal was the inheritance she now has. I've written the authorities in Dauphin County to see if I can get more of a handle on her past."

****

The day had turned gray and dismal with a bit of drizzle and chill in the air. Before long that drizzle would be replaced by snow. I wasn't ready for that yet. I was hurrying back to my office when I heard someone coming up behind me. I spun around.

"I've been all over town looking for you," said Jesse Ewing.

"You've been looking for me?" I asked Ewing, wondering why an officer on the Shannon police force was looking for me.

"Yeah. But how about we go in your office to discuss it?" he asked, throwing his arms around himself. "It's cold out here."

I escorted him inside and poured us both a cup of coffee. "Sorry. I don't have any cream," I told him.

"Not to worry. I prefer it black."

"So, what's this about?"

Ewing took a sip of his coffee, sat the cup down on my desk and looked up at me. "You know a man named Reilly?"

"No. But I was told there was one of that name looking for me yesterday."

"Well you won't be talking to him—at least not in this lifetime."

"What? Whadya mean?"

"Dead," Ewing said. "He was found last night behind the livery stable just down the street from the courthouse. You know the one I mean."

I nodded. "The one I always use when I go to your fair city." Though I already had a suspicion, I asked, "What happened to him?"

"Someone slit his throat. At first we thought it a robbery, but..."

"You found a message from me in his pocket?"

Ewing cocked an eye at me. "Eh?"

I explained what I'd learned about the man's arrival in Arahpot and the message alleged from me. "I sent no such message. I didn't even know the man had come looking for me until yesterday afternoon. Who was he anyway?"

Ewing slurped coffee and gave me another quizzical glance. "You're sure you didn't know anything about him?"

"I said not. Who was he?"

"He worked for a detective agency."

A light dawned. "The Casey Agency?"

"Right."

"Did he happen to have a photograph on him?"

"No. Nothing but his personal papers, identification, a small roll of money and the note led us to you. As soon as we saw the money we knew it hadn't been a robbery. What's this about a photograph?"

I told him about Runkle and the connection to the Casey agency.

"Hmph," Ewing muttered, tugging at an earlobe. "So while you were unaware of the detective's arrival here your chameleon Potteiger must have spied him, sent him a spurious message to lure him to Shannon where he dispatched him. I find it hard to believe, but it must be what happened."

I nodded. "I can't understand why Reilly responded to a note from a man who wasn't expecting him."

"Maybe he'd been led to believe you were. You had no notice from his superiors?"

"None I was aware of. Let's go over to the telegraph office. I have to notify Kelly anyway."

****

"Why should a gouty man make his will?" Gutshall asked for the second time.

None of us responded, earning us a scowl from the man. We were gathered—he, Emma, Lydia and I in my parlor, a change from our usual location at the Longlow residence. Despite a reluctance to participate in frivolities in light of pressing duty and responsibilities, I felt an obligation to repay Lydia for the many meals she'd hosted recently. I'd ordered a meal from the hotel for the four of us and had it delivered to my place.

The hotel sent over boiled pork, beans, potatoes and greens along with a lemon pie for dessert. It was adequate fare, though definitely not so tasty as Lydia might have provided. I was content to have the evening end with the meal but Gutshall insisted we should continue with some game or other. When no one suggested a better, he came up with the idea of Conundrums.

"Must I repeat it again?" he asked now when none of us answered. "Can no one guess the answer? It's simple when you give it a little thought. *To have his legatees*. Get it? His leg-at-ease."

"I'm sorry, Cyrus. I just can't concentrate tonight. Too much else on my mind," I told him.

He thought a moment. Then sensing the source of my distraction, asked, "So Casey had sent you a message to expect his man Reilly?"

"Yes. Only I never got it. The telegrapher said his lad pinned a note to my door, directing me to come to his office. I found no such note and never went."

Lydia shivered and gripped my forearm. "Then this man Potteiger must be walking among us unrecognized," she said. "It's frightening to think this killer could be someone we encounter daily and don't recognize for what he is."

"Ewing called him a chameleon," I said. "It seems accurate. He passes himself off as someone innocent and we rub shoulders with him unaware of the danger he poses."

"Frightening," Emma said.

"If only we knew what he looked like," Gutshall said, taking advantage of the opportunity to throw an arm about Emma's shoulders. She didn't object and he drew her nearer.

The sight of it irritated me and I fought to keep it from showing in my expression. "Does anyone want more coffee?" I asked, seeking a means of distraction.

The girls declined but, of course, Gutshall voted for more.

"Is there still some in the pot?" Lydia asked, rising and coming with me. "I could make more if there isn't enough."

I was glad for her company and didn't care if there was coffee or not. Pleased to be alone, I took her in my arms as we entered the kitchen and tried for a kiss. "Hold on, sonny," she said, pushing me away at arms length. Then, before I could release her, Lydia folded back into my arms and raised her face to mine. Emboldened, I bent to meet her.

I tasted a hint of that lemon pie on her lips. Like a bee after nectar, I tried for another kiss. Lydia broke loose and turned away. She brushed down her skirt with her hands and crossed quickly to the stove. She picked up the coffee pot and gave it a shake. "I think there's enough here," she said.

"Lydia."

She raised a hand. "Don't say any more, Sylvester. Not now."

So I kept my mouth shut, sated for the moment with the affection granted.

It brought to mind the first time I'd kissed her. I'm one of those fellows with two left feet and dancing is not a pursuit I undertake without some misgiving. But I'd been pursuing the girl at a variety of social activities without affirmative answer to my desire to court her. Her father hinted Lydia had a liking for dance. So, the next time I learned of one in the area, I asked. I nearly fell over when she agreed to go with me.

I thought this would be like other country dances I'd been to and felt comfortable about it. But it proved a more cosmopolitan crowd and I soon found I was out of place. I managed to step on her toes so many times I was sure she'd never talk to me again. Lydia said not a word and smiled through it all. Glad for a break from all the glissades and hops, I got us some punch and sat one out. We managed a little conversation. I didn't know her well enough then to go full-stream. The next thing I knew the band struck up one of those polka waltzes and she seized my hand and said, "Come on," leading me back to the dance floor.

I didn't know what was expected of me but did the best I could, copying the moves of the man in front of me. A hop on the left foot, then back. Glissade and turn around. Then a hop on the right foot, forward and back. Another glissade. Lydia knew exactly what she was doing and guided me through it with barely a misstep, her beaming a big smile and hanging onto me. Round and round we went and I was so dizzy I nearly passed out before we made the second and third stages of the dance. We were near a darkened corner of the dance floor when it ended and she was laughing and giggling and looked so lovely I couldn't help myself. I kissed her.

That was the first time and we were a couple after that. I was in heaven, save for the fact she declined to marry me.

OCTOBER 22, 1897

CHAPTER 25

Raised voices drew my attention as I approached Matilda Rebuck's boarding house. Fearing the worst, I broke into a trot. Coming around the corner, I found Barbara Frey engaged in a verbal duel with Reverend Huber. Matilda leaned in the doorway, clutching Nick who hung onto her like a moth on a screen. "Hold!" I shouted. "What's going on here?"

They turned as one, both babbling at me. I couldn't tell what one was saying for the chatter of the other. I raised a hand. "One at a time. Barbara."

"But..." the minister started.

"You'll get your turn, Reverend. Ladies first."

His dark eyes scoured me but he held his tongue.

"Go on, Barbara," I coaxed.

She gave Huber a scathing look, then turned her attention to me. "I found him skulking about this morning."

"I wasn't skulking," the minister said, flushing. "I was..."

I raised my hand again and nodded for Barbara to continue.

"He was peeking in the kitchen window," she said. "If that isn't skulking I don't know what is. When Matilda opened the door and shouted at him he said he was looking for Nick."

"He wants to take the boy away," Matilda chimed in.

"I'm only looking out for his..."

"Reverend, I'm not going to tell you again. You will have your opportunity to give your side of things."

Huber snapped his mouth shut with an audible click of his teeth. He hung his head and dug the toe of his boot into the cinders of the driveway. The man stood, his fists clenching and unclenching at his side.

I nodded to Barbara.

"He said it wasn't a fit place for the boy—with us. Like we're not decent folk, like those who go to his church. Where's he get off, saying things like that?"

I turned back to Huber and indicated he should speak. His gaze swept from me to the women. "I meant no harm. I was only considering the welfare of the boy. I heard what happened to his mother and that he was staying here. I knocked at the door..."

"Liar!" Matilda squeaked.

I gave her a cautioning glance.

"I did," Huber went on. "Perhaps they didn't hear. That's when I went to the window—to see if anyone was about. This woman," and he pointed at Matilda, "came out, screaming like a virago..."

"See," Matilda blurted, "he's calling me names again."

"I'm sorry," Huber said, whirling to her. "I meant no harm. It was just—you wouldn't listen to reason."

"Reason?" Matilda said, looking up at me. "He'd put the boy in some orphanage. A place where he'd be one of many. Here he's with friends of his mother. A place where he's assured of some love and tenderness." She glanced at her daughter on saying this last and I saw where the boy would find the greatest affection. Nick was still hanging onto Matilda, though his eyes were fixed on the minister with a mix of fear and loathing.

"I'm sure your intentions were well-meant, Reverend," I said. "But I'd think a Christian should show more charity than judgment toward others."

His gaze snapped to me. "As I said, I meant no harm." He flashed a mechanical smile. "I may have said some things in haste better left unsaid. My only concern is for the welfare of the boy."

"Well, I think the lad should have some say in what's done. What do you think, Nick? Do you want to stay here or go with Reverend Huber?"

Nick swallowed. He looked from me to Huber and back again. "I want to stay here," he said.

Huber started to say something more when there came a clatter behind us. We turned and saw a buckboard coming up the road toward us. As it drew nearer I saw Christopher Kintzler was driving and Catherine Deibert sat beside him, a portmanteau on her lap. Kintzler had replaced his fancy hat with a plain wool cap, but he still wore his muffler.

Huber jammed his hat down on his head and strode off without a backward glance.

Kintzler pulled up at the gate and halted his horse. He jumped off the wagon, went around and helped Catherine down. She came slowly toward us, carrying her bag. Kintzler got a small trunk from the wagon bed and followed. As they passed, he darted a shy look at Barbara who did her best to ignore him.

"Your room is ready, Miss Deibert," Matilda said, smiling.

"Good morning, Miss Catherine," I said, doffing my cap. "You're staying here?"

"Temporarily," she said. "Until I can find a house to rent. What was *he* doing here?" she asked, staring after Huber.

"A little misunderstanding," I told her.

"Misunderstanding, my foot," Matilda snapped. "He was up to no good."

"I can believe that," Catherine said. "Will you show me to my room? Come along, Christopher."

They went off together and I turned back to Barbara. "Mind if I have a word with Nick?"

"Of course not. I'll be inside."

I sat on the stoop and signaled for the boy to join me.

"Are you afraid of that man?"

He shook his head.

"Are you sure? I saw the way you looked at him. You can tell me, Nick. I won't let him hurt you. Has he harmed you or threatened you in the past?"

The boy was quiet for a moment, head bent, hands on his knees, one leg jiggling. Finally, he mumbled, "My Ma told me to keep away from him."

"Why?"

"I dunno. She never said. We saw him one time when we was out together. That's when she said it. I could tell she didn't like him. I think she was afraid of him."

"Did she say why?"

He shook his head. "She didn't say she was scared of him. I just thought she might be. I could tell she didn't like him and I figured she might be afraid because of what she told me."

"Do you think he might have been the man she went to see that night?"

The boy gave me a puzzled look. "Why would she go see him? She never went to church. What business would she have with him?"

That was a question I couldn't answer. It was his remark about her fear prompted the question. I didn't conceive of Lizzie being a church-goer and maybe her dislike of the man was nothing more than a reaction to the attitude he'd displayed toward Barbara and Matilda.

Barbara came to the door then. "Are you done with Nick?"

"Nothing else you want to tell me, boy?"

Nick shook his head.

"I suppose so."

"Okay." Barbara ruffled the boy's hair. "The lady has some errands. You want to help?" Getting a nod of assent, she told him to go on inside. Once he'd gone, she turned back to me. "He's not going back to Beiler's. He can stay here and earn his keep with a few chores."

"That's fine. I think he's better off here, too. Are you going to let him attend school?"

She shrugged. "If he wants. It's free, haint it? Don't see no reason not to let him."

Catherine Deibert came out before I left. "Has your sister-in-law put you out?" I asked.

"She hasn't spoke two words to me since Valentine's funeral. Not that I care. I have no desire to speak to her, either. And I decided I didn't want to stay out there and watch her and that excuse for a minister carrying on."

"Huber?"

"The very one. The man is a scoundrel—not fit to wear the cloth. If his parishioners were aware of the way he has carried on with that woman with her husband barely in the ground. It's disgusting."

"Do you think there was something between them while your brother was alive?"

She shook her head. "If there was, I didn't see it. I mean he was there every day but they were discrete in our presence. Now it's apparent they don't care what I might think or feel."

I wondered if the minister knew of my suspicions about his lover.

****

"How dare you?" Huber snapped, his expression that of a man who's found a fly in his soup. "You accuse Mrs. Deibert of poisoning her husband and now you imply I was a party to the deed." His face turned purple as he spoke and his eyes looked as though they might pop out of their sockets.

Though hardly an admission, his reaction showed I'd touched a nerve.

"There's evidence Mrs. Deibert had access to arsenic, which killed her husband. And, you have to admit, you've been very close to the lady, Reverend."

Huber grunted. "Evidence? Verbena explained why she had arsenic. She's told me what passed between you. I've advised her to have the lawyer, Berkheimer, caution you. There is such a thing as slander, you know. Valentine's death was surely accidental. Even you can't be so dense as not to have realized the man's history of self-medication. And, as to my own behavior—I won't have you tarnish my good name with such blatant fabrications. Of course I'm close to the woman. I've been her tutor, a position for which her husband hired me. And it was he named me executor of his will. That was not my choice, but it is an obligation I take seriously."

"I'm sure you do." I didn't take lightly his threat about the attorney. Berkheimer had said nothing to me, but the threat of a libel suit would earn me no grace in McLean Ruppenthal's opinion. Still, I had to pursue my instincts. "But you have to admit, a lot of judgments are made on the basis of appearances. You've been guilty of that yourself."

"If you're talking about those women, my judgment was based on more than appearance. If you were doing your job such behavior would not be tolerated in this community."

"I've had more complaints about some of your parishioners than I have about those women. Barbara Frey will take good care of young Nick. You needn't worry on his account. She's even promised to send him back to school—something his own mother wasn't willing to do."

"Commendable," he said, with a snort. His gaze flicked over me again and he asked, "Are you done with me now?"

I nodded. "At least for the time being."

****

"Surely you can't believe he was involved," Lydia said.

"No one is above suspicion," I told her, "not even a man of the cloth."

"Well I can't believe it. I think you're jumping to conclusions just because you don't like the man."

"Liking him or not has nothing to do with it." I pushed my plate aside and loosened my belt. Lydia had fixed us another fine lunch at the store and I was explaining the morning's events to her. She'd listened in rapt attention until I came down to my most recent encounter with her minister.

"But you admit you don't like the man."

"I think he's a sneaky, smarmy individual. I'm not saying he was directly involved in Deibert's murder. But I think he knows more than he's saying."

****

The drumming of footsteps behind me and I whirled around. The footsteps rattled through fallen leaves and slowed. I peered into the dark and vaguely made out a small form against the pale glow of a white-washed fence. "Who's there?" I called out.

The figure took a hesitant step forward. "Sheriff? That you?"

He moved out of the shadows into the radiance of the street lamp.

"Nick?"

"I was looking for you. Miss Longlow said you went home."

"That's where I was headed. What is it, boy?"

He approached and I saw his pale face streaked with dried tears. His eyes blinked and he gnawed at his lower lip. "You gotta come," he said in a low voice.

I laid a hand on his thin shoulder. "What's the matter, Nick? You're shaking like a leaf."

The boy looked up at me. "Somebody came in the room. I think they meant to hurt Miss Barbara."

Nick explained as we hurried to the boarding house. He and Barbara had gone to bed. She was letting him sleep in her room since the boy was experiencing night-fears. Nick had just drifted off to sleep when he was awakened by Barbara's scream. She was struggling with a figure hovering over the bed. "Go for help," she'd called to him. "Get Sheriff Tilghman."

Lights were blazing in the downstairs windows of the house as Nick and I approached. Fearing the worse, I opened the door and called out, "Barbara. Matilda!" I turned to Nick. "Where's her room? Show me."

Nick led me down the hall. A door stood ajar at the end and I heard voices. Female voices. I poked my head in the doorway.

Barbara sat on her bed, Matilda on one side of her and Catherine Deibert on the other. Barbara looked up and gave me a weak smile as I entered. "Are you okay?"

She nodded. "He got scared off," she told me.

"Do you know who it was? Did you get a look at him?"

She shook her head. "I woke and he was bending over me. I couldn't see who it was in the dark. When I screamed for Nick to get you he put a hand over my mouth."

"We must have scared him off," Catherine said. "Matilda and I heard the girl screaming and we both came from our rooms. The man ran out the back door as we came down the stairs."

"Boarders or not," Matilda said, "these doors are going to be locked from now on when we go to bed."

"That's a good idea, Tillie," I told her. "I'm glad you're all right," I added, turning to Barbara. "Too bad you couldn't see who it was."

Barbara gave a brave smile. "Well I scratched him good," she said.

"And I found this," Matilda said, holding up a polka dot muffler.

OCTOBER 23, 1897

CHAPTER 26

"It's yours, isn't it?"

Christopher Kintzler clutched the muffler to his chest and nodded. He raised his eyes and gazed at me with a look like a chastened puppy. "I meant her no harm."

"No harm? You meant to kill her like you did Runkle. I've got the goods on you this time, mister. You're going back to jail and this time there'll be no pardon." I'd assumed the danger to Barbara was past and Lizzie had been the one in trouble all along. Now I wasn't so sure. And my doubts about young Kintzler had risen again.

"No! I never." He raised a hand and touched the raw scratch marks on his cheek and neck. "I'd never hurt Barbara. I swear it. And I didn't kill that other man, neither. Why would I? I didn't even know him."

"Where's your wife? I need to talk to her, too, Phoebus."

"What?" He gave me a quizzical look. "I told you, my wife left me. I don't know where she is. Why are you calling me Phoebus? You know who I am."

"I know who I thought you were. Maybe you've become something worse. You're telling me you don't know the name Phoebus Potteiger?"

"Potteiger? No. Why should I know that name? It doesn't mean a thing to me."

Ollie Kintzler rose from his rocker. He came and stood between us. "He's telling the truth, Sheriff. Barbara Frey is the last person on earth my boy would hurt."

"Oh?" I said, turning to him. "Why should I believe that?"

Kintzler looked from me to his son and back again. "Because the boy has been in love with her since they were children." He hung his head. "Maybe if I wouldn't have interfered he might have married her and not that other one and his life would have turned out different."

"It wasn't your fault, Pa."

"Yes. It was. If I'd let the two of you alone your life and hers would have been better."

"You don't know that."

"Okay," I interrupted. "I'm feeling like the odd man out here. One of you explain to me what you're talking about."

"What Pa said—I love Barbara. I always have. I courted her back when we was younger. But Matilda, her mother, and Pa, they never liked one another and they came between us. I went away and tried to forget her. I married Sylvia and it was wrong, because I never loved her."

"So what were you doing in Barbara's room last night?"

"I just wanted to talk to her—to see if we could start over."

"The boy's tried to talk to her several times since he got back," Ollie put in.

"She thinks I wouldn't want her because of the things she's done since we broke up. She won't believe I don't care about none of that. I just wanted to talk to her. I swear it."

"So why sneak into her room at night?"

"I thought if I could just talk to her alone I might..."

"How'd you know which room was hers?"

Christopher dipped his head, embarrassed. "I guess I been peeking in windows at night. But I wasn't sure which was the right room until yesterday when Miss Deibert hired me to help her move and I took her to the house. I was coming out and I saw Barbara go in the room. She was carrying wash—personal things—so I knew that must be her room."

Looking at his pathetic expression I wanted to believe him. But I couldn't be sure. Instinct was itching at me again. If I was a swearing man I'd have swore just then. I was burdened with too many crimes and too many suspects. "All right," I said finally, "I'm going to talk to Barbara. If she backs up your story I might be inclined to believe you."

"Thank you, Sheriff," Christopher said, a half-smile twitching at his lips.

"You're not off the hook yet. She could still press charges you know."

"Why would she do that?" the old man asked.

I spun on him. "Love or not, what your son did is called breaking and entering. It's a crime—at least it was last time I looked."

****

Turn out for Elizabeth Kline's funeral was light compared to that for Conrad Runkle and Valentine Deibert. Her son, Nick, Matilda Rebuck and Barbara Frey were the main mourners. Cyrus Gutshall, Emma Mariner, Lydia and I made up the rest of those attending—unless you counted the grave diggers and a murder of crows circling in the pines on the edge of the community cemetery.

The whole affair was held there in the cemetery. There was no crepe and the only flowers were a small frost-nipped bouquet picked earlier that morning by Nick and Barbara. It was a sad affair and I thought it a bit much to have attended three funerals in one month.

At least the weather was decent. The sun shone brightly in a near cloudless sky, the air was tolerably warm and birds sang to the accompaniment of the cawing of the crows.

There was no minister. The mourners wouldn't have wanted Huber and, since they weren't church-goers, had no idea who else to ask. In lieu of clergy, Lydia read a short passage from scripture and those of us who'd known Lizzie spoke a few words in memory.

Matilda had donated the lot. I presumed that was at the urging of Barbara and not a simple gesture of charity. Despite protests to the contrary, Matilda Rebuck was well-off and could afford the cost of the lot, the undertaker and the other necessary amenities. Still I had broached the subject to the Mariners of taking up a collection as had been done in Runkle's behalf. Clara thought it a commendable idea and said she'd do what she could to organize it. Our interest was not in repaying Matilda but in laying up something for the boy's security. I'm proud to say Lydia was the first to contribute.

And, when the brief service concluded, Lydia went over to Matilda and suggested we all go to the hotel for a memorial luncheon. Matilda gave her a startled look and couldn't seem to get her mouth to working.

"You hadn't planned a meal yourself, had you?" Lydia asked.

Matilda sputtered and found her voice. "No. I didn't think of it."

"It's a wonderful idea," Barbara said, laying a hand on Lydia's arm.

"I-I..." Matilda stuttered.

"Don't worry about the cost," I added. "We're all prepared to chip in."

That relieved Matilda of her anxiety and she gave her consent as well.

After the meal (which again was adequate but not up to the standards I was used to) I managed to get a moment alone with Barbara.

"Did you know the man who accosted you was Christopher Kintzler?"

Barbara lowered her eyes. "Not until I saw the scarf he left behind."

"So why didn't you say so?"

She raised her eyes and looked at me. "I didn't want to get him in trouble. He's had enough bad luck. I was relieved when I recognized his muffler. I knew he meant me no harm."

"That was his claim. The two of you seem to have a history I was unaware of."

"In the past," she said, lowering her head again.

"Do you think him capable of murder?"

Her head jerked up, eyes widening in shock.

"Do you think he's the one killed Runkle and Lizzie?"

"No. Of course not. Why would he do that? Christopher's not a bad man. He's not the kind to go around hurting people."

"He had a knife the night he got in the brawl with Wes Graeff."

Barbara shrugged her thin shoulders. "So? Lots of men in Arahpot carry knives. That don't mean they go sticking them in folks."

"True. Does the name Phoebus Potteiger mean anything to you?"

She gave me a quizzical look. "You asked me that before. I said not."

"What about Kintzler's wife? What do you know about her?"

"Not much. We never met. His Pa said she got a divorce when Christopher went to jail."

"Do you want to press charges against him?"

"Against Christopher? For what?"

"Breaking and entering. It is a crime."

She shook her head. "He meant no harm."

"I'd like to believe that, but he's still a suspect in the other crimes."

"I told you, Christopher would never harm anyone. He's a good man."

"Do you still have feelings for him, Barbara?"

The girl scowled. "It's too late for that."

"Maybe. Maybe not." I hadn't failed to notice the glow in her eyes or the catch in her voice whenever his name was mentioned. "He seems to still care about you. He said you refuse to talk to him."

"There's nothing to talk about."

"He seems to think there is. He said that's why he came to your room. Why don't you talk to him?"

Barbara turned and started to walk away. "What's past is past. There's nothing more to be said."

I wasn't so sure of that. Despite the possibility I might find him guilty of more heinous crimes than trying to speak to a girl he obviously still loved, I couldn't help but hope there might yet be time for them to renew their relationship. I suppose it's just the romantic in me.

Lydia was waiting for me by the main door of the dining room. "You two seem back to your coziness," she said with a smile as I came up to her.

"It had to do with the case."

"Of course," she said, taking my arm. "Are you going to walk me back to the store?"

"That I am. Where are the others?" I asked, referring to Cyrus and Emma.

"Emma had to get back to work. Cyrus escorted her. They make a lovely couple, don't you think?"

A compliant nod was the best I could manage in response. We walked out onto the sunlit street, Lydia holding my arm with one hand and clutching her bible in the other. We nodded to acquaintances along the way, passing a word or two with some, and reached the store in too short a time. "Will I see you tonight?" I asked, hopefully

"Have you forgotten what day it is?" she said with a broad smile.

I scratched my pate. "It's Saturday."

"Yes. The twenty-third. The Harvest Festival at the church. Did you forget you promised to take me?"

Going to a church festival—especially one where Huber was pastor—wasn't something I normally would have jumped at. But, since I was escorting the prettiest girl in town, I expected I could bear it. "Of course not. Just in all the confusion..."

"You did forget," she chided. "But I'll forgive you." She kissed my cheek.

"What time should I pick you up. Will there be food?"

"Of course there'll be food, silly." She slapped my arm. "Around six would be fine."

"Okay. See you then." I started off.

"Sylvester."

"Yes?"

"That was really a nice idea of yours, starting the fund for the boy."

****

Now you might consider it hypocritical, but the Harvest Festival is one occasion when you can't keep me away from church.

Ours is normally held in September. But with the leaving of one pastor and the coming of another, this year the congregation had voted to hold it in October and as an alternative to Halloween, which some see as pagan, though I've always considered it just a good time for children.

Because of our dependence on agriculture, Harvest Festival is important to us. No matter when it's observed, Harvest Festival in Arahpot means a thanksgiving service in appreciation of God's gifts, crowds of people having a good time, crafts on display, homemade soups and plenty of tasty baked goods.

Underlying all the religious and social veneer though, the real purpose of the festival is to raise money. And to that end, in most years it's uncommonly successful.

This appeared to be no exception as we came in and saw the throngs of people lined up at stands and circulating around booths in the church community rooms. "Will you look at that," said Albert Casey, gawking at a display of home-made pastries.

"Does your church observe a harvest celebration, Mr. Casey?" Lydia asked.

Casey, who was as tall as me but thin as a fence post, gave her a toothy grin. "I haven't been to Mass or confession in so long they might have changed. But, in my memory, they have nothing to compare in the amount of delicious-looking food. Is there always so much?"

"More than enough to satisfy the needs of men such as us," I said, delighted to be acquainted with another who admired good victuals as much as me. Casey had been waiting at my office when I returned that afternoon and I soon took a liking to the ebullient Irishman. A man in his mid-forties, he had a florid complexion, a bushy red mustache and goatee, a loud voice and a forthright manner.

He brought with him a police photograph of Phoebus Potteiger, which he'd finally found after learning from me of the murder of his associate, Reilly. "Do you know the man?"

It took no more than a glance. "Oh, I do indeed. Yes. I know him." It sent a thrill through me to know at last who was responsible for all the recent misery visited on my town. It was a surprise, but not a shock, looking on his features in that poorly-lit, dark image. Casey said the photograph had been taken when the man was a suspect in another case but there had not been enough evidence to hold him in that instance.

"Do you know where to find him?"

"I do. And you and I shall apprehend him in due time. But first I want you to join me and my friend for supper."

Casey looked at me in surprise. "Don't you want to go now? Aren't you afraid he'll get away?"

"Not to worry. He's not going anywhere for the present. We're going to give him a surprise tonight, my friend."

So I convinced him to join Lydia and me at the Harvest Festival. I introduced him as a visiting detective but didn't fill her in on the purpose of his call. I thought the arrest of Phoebus Potteiger later that night would be a fitting surprise for her as well.

"Have you been to Arahpot before, Mr. Casey?" she asked now.

"I have not. It seems a pleasant place, particularly if all its denizens prove as friendly as you and Sheriff Tilghman."

"You're very kind, sir. We do try to be welcoming to visitors. Am I being too forward if I recommend a piece of that apple pie there, since I'm the one made it."

"I can testify you'll find it first-rate," I told him.

We made our way around the room, sampling various fare and

remarking on the quality of various quilts, woodwork and other crafts, introducing Casey to people along the way. We were having a second bowl of oyster stew when I spied Reverend Huber enter the room, accompanied by Verbena Deibert.

Lydia spotted them at the same time. "I'd say it was a bit bold of her to be out in public so soon after her husband's death," she said. "And look, she doesn't even have the decency to wear mourning clothes for a respectable period."

She was right. Verbena was clad in a handsome lavender waist of taffeta silk and a gray Oxford skirt with sateen plaiting round the bottom. An elegant outfit for the occasion and I might have added the way she clung to Huber had naught to do with spiritual support.

Huber gave a start and halted in mid-step when he saw us.

"Well I'll be," Casey said, dropping his spoon.

"Hello, Phoebus," I said, going forward and gripping the man by the forearm. "Nice of you to join us. Aren't you going to introduce us to your wife?"

CHAPTER 27

Reverend Leonard Huber, whom we now knew to be Phoebus Potteiger, released his companion's arm and spun round, looking for a way out. Verbena, equally surprised but apparently not as flustered, dipped a hand into her reticule and drew out one of those short-barreled bicycle revolvers, which she pointed at me. "Let go of his arm," she threatened, "or I will shoot you."

I believed the woman. She had that intense, determined expression which usually means business. I let go of Potteiger's arm and angled myself in front of Lydia. No way I wanted her getting shot. Casey took a step forward and Verbena swiveled the barrel of her gun in his direction. The detective stopped, stood nibbling his mustache. People around us stared aghast, wondering what was going on. For a long moment there wasn't a sound in the room, not a whisper of conversation nor clink of silverware.

"Why don't you put that weapon away, Verbena," I said. "No use making a bad situation worse."

She grinned. "I think the situation's worse for you than us. We are going to leave now." And she started backing up.

Potteiger drew a long-bladed knife from his sleeve and waved it in my direction. "You have more lives than a cat, Tilghman. You've spoiled everything. This was meant to be our retirement."

"Shut up," Verbena told him. "Let's just get out of here."

Cyrus Gutshall stepped out of the crowd then and stuck the barrel of the pistol I'd given him between Verbena's shoulder blades. "I don't think you're going anywhere, lady," he told her. "Drop the gun."

Her face contorted by an ugly frown, Verbena complied.

Potteiger whirled around but before he could raise his knife I'd locked onto him again and twisted his arm behind his back. He howled and twisted trying to get loose but I held on until he dropped the knife.

"Do you have your manacles, Mr. Casey?"

"I do." And he stepped forward, snapping one link round Verbena's slim wrist and securing Potteiger with the other.

Startled, members of the congregation and the community milled about us, confused by what had just happened. "Sheriff Tilghman," one aged woman asked, "why are you arresting our pastor?"

"Because he's fallen from grace," I told her. "Boys, would you mind escorting our prisoners down to the lock up?" I said to Gutshall and Casey. "I'll be there directly."

As they went off, Lydia looked up at me and said with a smile, "You've made..."

"Cyrus my deputy," I confirmed with a nod. I still wasn't thrilled with the man, but he was the best applicant I'd had in a long while. A man can't wait for ever when he knows he needs help.

CHAPTER 28

Our little town was abuzz with plenty of fuel for gossip in the following days. It wasn't often we had so much excitement in such a short period of time. I supposed it would be some time before we had another Harvest Festival to match this one.

Phoebus Potteiger wasn't shy about filling in the details of his crimes. He knew when the game was up. Verbena wasn't quite so forthcoming. Maybe she thought a jury would take her gender into consideration as they did in the case of Lizzie Borden and be lenient toward her if she held onto her demure and complaisant manner.

I had my doubts about that. Her husband implicated her in everything. I suspect he didn't intend to be the only one wearing a hemp necktie.

According to the story he told, the couple had gone on the run after fleecing Runkle of a bundle down in Lancaster County. They agreed to separate temporarily in hope that would throw any pursuers off the scent. Verbena had gone alone to Dauphin County and there she'd met poor Valentine Deibert. The man proved an easy mark and Verbena had no difficulty convincing him to marry her in a quick ceremony before a justice of the peace.

"I had nothing to do with it," Potteiger confessed to me. "Perhaps she intended to forget about me and forge a new life for herself." He grinned and gave a little shrug. "Despite appearances to the contrary, she is a devious and independent creature. You may not believe it, but she has been the architect of some of our best schemes."

I didn't doubt it. After spending some time interviewing the two of them I came to the realization Verbena was much the smarter of the two.

Potteiger said he eventually learned of her move and formulated a plan to reunite with her. "Despite her faults," he said, "I love the girl."

"So how did you arrange to become pastor of the church here?"

"Purely by chance," he said, grinning again. "I was on the road one night, heading for your county, when I encountered a fellow traveler. We agreed to ride together, since we were going in the same direction. It wasn't my intent originally to harm the fellow. Honest. I just sought some companionship. But, as we rode along, he told me the purpose of his journey."

"And you killed him and took his place?"

"I did. Fortunately he was a bachelor with no family to come visiting him. The people here had never met him. It was a perfect set up."

"But how were you able to fill the duties of a minister? I mean, your background..."

Potteiger laughed. "My father was a Methodist minister. I'm well acquainted with that life and occupation. Have you not heard tales about the children of ministers? They're true, you know. And, next to a lawyer, there's no profession easier to emulate. All it takes is to exhibit a pious front and have a garrulous nature."

I was amazed at the man's candor. "And you have no qualms about murdering innocent people?"

He snorted with laughter. "None. Who is to say who is more innocent than another? All must die at some point. If another's need is furthered by my death wouldn't they make the same choices I did?"

"I don't think everyone places such little value on the life of others. I believe I can understand why you killed Runkle. He was a threat to you. But why was it necessary to kill poor Lizzie? What threat..."

"Why, the same, man." And he smiled. "She was equally a threat. Runkle had confided in her. She knew about us and wanted money to keep quiet."

"Lizzie did? She told me she'd had no dealings with Runkle. Why would he have confided in her?"

"Oh, Sheriff. You are an innocent, aren't you? The girl was a whore. Do you think she was going to tell you the truth when she hoped to profit by her knowledge of us?"

"Then why did you send Barbara and not her to summon Runkle from the tavern that night? Wouldn't he have come out for Lizzie?"

Potteiger nodded. "He might have. But it was Lizzie's idea to send the Frey girl. That way she wasn't implicated if you questioned the events of that night. I thought that quite wise of her."

"Why was it Verbena and not you summoned him that night?"

"Don't you see? He didn't fear Verbena. He knew she was my wife but, like you, he imagined her docile, a mere pawn in my plotting. The fool came out unarmed to talk to her. I hoped to have done with him quickly but he put up more of a fight than I expected."

What he said made sense. Runkle had left his revolver in his coat and gone outside to meet with Verbena, not expecting Potteiger to attack him from the shadows. The man hadn't stood a chance against these schemers.

Potteiger answered any questions I put to him with a forthrightness that sickened me. There were a few questions only Verbena could answer. I tried once more after their arraignment and while we awaited their trial in the next session of court.

"You're surely going to prison," I said, standing outside her cell. "You may even hang. Wouldn't you like to clear your conscience?"

She sat on her bunk, hands folded in her lap, and gazed up at me with no expression showing on her pretty face. I thought she looked like one of those German china dolls. "Is that going to save me from the rope?" she asked, calmly.

"Perhaps it would help you accept your fate."

A thin smile parted her lips. "Really? Do you honestly think it makes dying any easier to explain your actions?"

I shrugged. "I can't really say. I'm not the one facing your fate."

"True. So, what is it you must know?"

"One thing that's puzzled me is why Valentine Deibert looked so frightened that day when he bumped into Runkle at the store. If he didn't know who Runkle was..."

She gave a little laugh. "He reacted to what I had told him of the man. We saw Runkle one day while we were still living in Dauphin County. The man didn't see us. I told Valentine Runkle was a man who'd wanted to marry me. I said I'd turned him down and he'd sworn vengeance, threatening to kill me. It helped convince him to move us away. When Runkle turned up here, Valentine thought he'd followed us."

"So why did he deny knowledge of him when I asked? If that's what he believed he could have requested protection from me."

"Yes. But then you might have talked to Runkle and he could have told you the truth. I expected that and convinced Valentine not to talk to you. I told him we could offer Runkle money to go away. He never knew about my meeting with the man. When you informed him Runkle had been stabbed the fool thought it was the work of thieves. He never guessed at our involvement."

"And what of Valentine? Did you poison him?"

Verbena turned away then, declining further conversation.

I suppose it really didn't matter. The two of them would pay for their crimes whether they admitted them or not.

DECEMBER 23, 1897

EPILOGUE

Time has passed. Phoebus and Verbena Potteiger have paid for their crimes. Life goes on much as it has in the past in Arahpot.

Some few things have changed. Winter has descended upon us and a thick coating of snow covers the landscape in white outside my windows as I sit here this morning nursing a second cup of coffee.

Cyrus Gutshall is officially my deputy and I've become a bit more accustomed to the man, though I could do without those tales of his derring-do in the Wild West. I have actually grown a little fond of the man—which I would not admit to his face. He continues to court Emma Mariner and has been accepted into the affection of her family, even that of Hiram.

Barbara Frey did finally relent and listen to what Christopher Kintzler had to say. I'm pleased to report they renewed their relationship and have recently wed. I even got to give the bride away. The two of them have also taken steps to adopt young Nick and plan to raise him as their son. Matilda surprised me by saying she was happy about the whole affair and sorry it had taken her so long to realize what a good man Christopher is.

Catherine Deibert has rightfully inherited her brother's property and has moved back to the farmhouse. She offered to hire Christopher and

Barbara to work for her but Barbara told me they intend leaving the area to escape wagging tongues who still see virtue in gossip.

Lydia is busier than ever, running the store, caring for her parents, handling the mail and continuing her church and social activities.

As for me, I've had another offer of a job in Shannon, which I turned down. Albert Casey also said he had a place for me in his agency any time I wanted. I was gratified by that, but I'm content to continue as sheriff of Arahpot. I do have a deputy now and my workload is a little lighter.

Oh, and in case you're wondering, I did propose to Lydia again.

She said she's thinking on it, which is more progress than I'd made in the past.

I guess you'd say that's cause for optimism.

The End

ABOUT THE AUTHOR

A retired newspaper editor, J. R. Lindermuth lives and writes in central Pennsylvania. Since his retirement he has served as librarian of his county historical society where he assists patrons with research and genealogy. He has published eight other novels, including four in his Sticks Hetrick mystery series. His short stories and articles have appeared in a variety of magazines, both print and on line. He is the father of two children and has four grandsons.

You are invited to visit his website at http://jrlindermuth.com

CPSIA information can be obtained at www.ICGtesting.com
Printed in the USA
BVOW05s0254210915

418887BV00001B/79/P

9 781610 090117